JULIETTE FORREST

SCHOLASTIC

More magical adventures by Juliette Forrest:

Twister

The True Colours
of Coral Glen

For all those who

dream by day

Published in the UK by Scholastic, 2021
Euston House, 24 Eversholt Street, London, NW1 1DB
Scholastic Ireland, 89E Lagan Road, Dublin Industrial Estate,
Glasnevin, Dublin, D11 HP5F

Cover illustration by Beatriz Castro

ISBN 978 0702 30106 3

A CIP catalogue record for this book
is available from the British Library.

Printed by CPI Group (UK) Ltd, Croydon, CR0 4YY
Paper made from wood grown in sustainable forests
and other controlled sources.

1 3 5 7 9 10 8 6 4 2

www.scholastic.co.uk

CHAPTER 1

Jeannie cried out for me to run.

I knew from the wild look in Roxy Patterson's eyes, and by the way she was pushing her sleeves up, that it was time for a sharp exit. Otherwise she would thump me, and Roxy had hands the size of shovels.

Breaking through the circle of jostling girls who spat names in my face, I tore along the street, making heads turn, dogs bark and pigeons shed their feathers. I flung myself down some narrow steps to the road below, careful to avoid the uneven paving stones at the bottom that had sent me sprawling before.

Two old ladies in the middle of the pavement tutted as I vaulted over their shopping bags. A notebook fell out of my pocket and landed with a slap on the concrete, its pages fluttering, but there was no time to snatch it up. Over the wail of an ambulance in the distance, I could hear Roxy Patterson yelling my name.

I flew past the crowd at the bus stop, past the stall that sold wonky fruit and vegetables, past Vanity Hair and Barbecue Kings – the smell of shampoo and charred meat clashing in the air.

I turned my head. Roxy and her gang were closing in on me. Ever since she'd found out I couldn't dream at night, she'd made my life a misery. Cats can dream, dogs can dream, even hamsters can dream – but not me.

People who can't dream don't have brains, she had said to me. *And that makes you too stupid to be allowed.*

I gritted my teeth and sped up. I still had the bruises from when she had cornered me on my way to school last week.

I spied an open door to some flats and fled inside the close. Neon splashes of graffiti strobed as I bombed past them. At the end of the passageway, I jumped down some steps into the gardens and ducked behind a low wall, hoping I'd managed to lose them.

My stomach let out a loud growl and I pressed my arm against it an attempt to silence it. Today, after weeks of hiding, I had decided to go to the canteen. Jeannie had given me half of her sandwich and I was about to take a bite when she had kicked me under the table.

"Look out," Jeannie had said, but it was too late. Roxy was right next to me. She had knocked the sandwich out of my hand, on to the floor, and then stamped on it.

"I had the best dream last night," Roxy said. "I don't suppose you know what that's like, do you?"

One of the dinner ladies sensed trouble brewing and started towards us.

"I'll get you later, freak," Roxy had whispered into my ear. She had smiled at the dinner lady and strolled off.

And after school she had been waiting.

Leaves crackled behind me, and before I could turn, two hands grabbed my shoulders, hauling me to my feet.

"Gotcha," Roxy hissed.

I attempted to twist free, but Roxy was much bigger than me. In a flash, I undid my zip and wriggled out of my coat, leaving her holding it.

I dashed towards the end of the garden. One of her gang sprang out from behind a hedge and lunged at me. I swerved around her, heading for the ivy-clad wall. As I hauled myself up it, Roxy gripped on to my foot and I lashed out. There was a grunt as I kicked her in the face. I scrambled over the top of the wall and tumbled over the other side, landing on a heap of empty cardboard boxes by some recycling bins.

"You're for it now, freak show," shouted Roxy over the wall.

I got to my feet and stumbled back on to the main street, limping past two seagulls fighting over a chip. I hurried around the next corner into Hidden Lane, bashing into a traffic warden, who shouted at me to *watch where I was going*, but I was already halfway down the cobbled street. I could hear footsteps pounding. Roxy and her gang never gave up.

As I approached the Dream Store, the door was slightly ajar. Above it, stencilled in gold lettering, was: *Dreams come true with DreamDrops.*

It would be a *dream come true* if I could avoid being turned red, black, blue, yellow and green by Roxy Patterson.

The bell tinkled sweetly as I slipped inside and leaned hard against the door to close it. Outside, there was a rumble of footsteps as Roxy Patterson and her gang charged past, heading towards the lockups at the end of the street.

A pulse beat in my neck, and my throat was as dry as Shredded Wheat.

That had been way too close for comfort.

I steadied my breathing and began to look around. I'd never plucked up the courage to come inside before.

Not another soul was about: the lights were off and it was as quiet as a Sunday morning. With its high ceilings and long narrow floor, the shop was much bigger on the inside than it looked from the outside. The scent of toffee popcorn was intoxicating and made my stomach rumble again. Two wrought-iron staircases on either side of the store led to a mezzanine level where there were self-service checkouts and DreamDrops merchandise for sale.

For as long as I could remember, the store had sold every type of dream imaginable to children in Parradicehill. There were ordinary dreams – the ones most people had every night – and then there were DreamDrops dreams, which were the best, most exciting nightmare-free adventures you could ever wish for while sleeping. They were suck-your-cheeks-in expensive, but everyone at school had them because all I heard were kids going on and *on* and ON about them in class, in the canteen, on the playing field, in the library and during detention. I'd give my right arm for a dream. I'd give my left arm too. But because I couldn't, the drops were my only hope of ever having one. Unfortunately, there was no way my family could afford them, which Roxy Patterson loved pointing out to anyone who'd listen.

A movement caught my eye. In the large window display, six dark blue Galaxy Exploration DreamDrops bottles twinkled under bell jars. A 3D hologram of a spacewoman bounced around as though she was striding gravity-free on the surface of the moon, before being scooped up by a rocket ship. She then zoomed in between shooting stars and red planets that hula-hooped their purple neon rings.

I stepped forward. The floors and walls of the Dream Store were covered in square tiles that glowed a soft, cloudy white. Oversized bottles of DreamDrops sat on plinths dotted around the front of the room. Behind them, on white shelves, were hundreds of the real bottles, each one filled with tantalizing adventures. At the back of the shop was an empty space. I wondered what it was for.

I walked further into the store, and spotted an exquisite bottle in the shape of an elephant's head. I picked it up. Safari Adventure DreamDrops. I'd never seen anything so beautiful in my life. As I ran my finger gently over the stopper, the elephant flapped its ears and trumpeted. The drops rattled softly as I examined the khaki bottle, amazed at the raised outlines of lions, rhinos and hippos on the glass.

Cradling the bottle to me, I wished it was mine, because if I could finally have a dream, Roxy Patterson would stop picking on me and she'd have to go and find someone else to slap with her giant hands.

"The store is closed," said a voice behind me.

I whirled around, startled, and let go of the DreamDrops, which fell to the floor, snapping the elephant's trunk clean off. I dropped to my knees and scooped the pieces up, my cheeks burning hotter than a frying pan.

"Please leave it; I'll tend to it later." The man studied me as though I was an exhibit in a museum. He wore a faded dark green tartan suit and a bright orange shirt. His face was covered in wrinkles, like the skin on hot milk when it puckers up. He had eyes the same colour as whirlpools that swallow ships. A bird sat on his shoulder, but I wasn't sure if it was real because this was the Dream Store.

"I've never seen a blackbird with an orange beak and yellow and brown feathers before," I said.

"That's because she's not a blackbird. She's a

mynah bird," replied the man. "Sausage found me in Madagascar and hasn't left my side since."

"*Knickers,*" said the bird.

"*Language, Sausage!* The children love her, but when she's left in charge of the store they teach her new words, some more useful than others." He produced a Brazil nut and held it out for Sausage, who snapped it up.

Just at that moment I caught sight of Roxy Patterson outside, her face as red as a fresh cut, and I hid behind a plinth.

The old man's white eyebrows lowered as he followed my gaze. Roxy pressed her face up against the window.

The man and I waited in silence. Sausage was quiet too. Roxy banged on the glass and turned to scan the lane. "You're dead when I find you, Ollo," she roared before she stormed off.

"*Big knickers in a twist,*" squawked Sausage.

I straightened up and came out from behind the plinth.

The man looked at me for a moment. "Allow me to introduce myself," he said. "I'm Mr Tannis

Curley and I'm the owner of the Dream Store. Who might you be?" Mr Curley had a deep, velvety voice. I decided he would be really good at reading stories aloud.

"I'm . . . Ollo."

"Oh, you're Ollo." Mr Curley peered at me over the top of his glasses. "I'm afraid I'm in the middle of something urgent, and I'll have to ask you to leave."

I didn't want to leave. Roxy Patterson might be waiting for me in Hidden Lane.

"Would you like to buy some DreamDrops while you're here?" he asked.

I had no money, so I shook my head.

"Then I wonder," Mr Curley went on, "might you be able to assist me with something before you go?"

He brought out two small bottles from his jacket pocket: one was tall, thin and yellow and the other was small, round and blue. "Which scent should I perfume the Dream Store with next?"

"You want me to choose?" I asked, surprised.

He passed me the yellow bottle. I unscrewed the lid and sniffed.

"What do you smell?" said Mr Curley.

"Farty biscuits," cackled Sausage as she circled around the room, honking like a goose.

"Language, Sausage!" Mr Curley narrowed his eyes at her. The bird chuckled and landed on the floor, lighting up the square beneath her.

I closed my eyes and breathed in deeply, my nostrils filling with lemon, sugary meringue and buttery pastry. I licked my lips. "Lemon meringue pie, Mr Curley!"

"And the other one?"

I swapped the yellow bottle for the blue one and wafted it under my nose. I sighed at the delicious aroma of baked apple and spice. "Cinnamon apple pie! It's one of my favourites. My gran makes it every time I visit. It's so good, I always have double helpings with cream and then feel sick."

Mr Curley laughed. "Cinnamon apple pie it is, then! Thank you for your help, Ollo, but I really must ask you to leave now."

I walked slowly behind him to the door. Mr Curley opened it and poked his head outside. A breeze blew into the shop, knocking a card off the wall. It fluttered down and slid across the floor towards me, stopping right at my feet. I picked it up.

> *Part-time assistant wanted. Must have a vivid imagination. Warm smile preferable. (Not suitable for those allergic to feathers.)*

Imagine being lucky enough to work at the Dream Store, I thought as I gave the note to Mr Curley.

"I declare Hidden Lane free from marauding girls," he said, pinning the card back on the wall. "It has been a pleasure meeting you."

"Oh no it wasn't!" piped up Sausage from his shoulder.

Mr Curley ignored the bird. "Next time you visit, Sausage and I will endeavour to match you with your perfect dream."

My heart near broke. Even though I wanted the drops more than anything, I wouldn't be back because I couldn't afford them.

"Thanks, Mr Curley."

I left the shop and he bolted the door behind me. I stood for a second and placed my hand against the window as I watched the spacewoman zooming around and the shooting stars arc and fizzle until I could bear it no more. I turned away and traipsed back along Hidden Lane, sighing heavily.

In the distance, I could see the high-rise I lived in sprouting up from Parradicehill's town centre like a weird growth. I looked at my watch and did a double take when I saw it was half past six.

I was late for dinner! Mum would be furious.

Hastening home, I spotted my coat in a puddle at the side of the road where Roxy must have chucked it. I picked it up and wrung it out. I knew for certain having a dream was the one thing I wanted most in the world and that I'd stop at nothing to make it happen.

CHAPTER 2

A bunch of kids kicked a football around in the car park across the road. Even though Roxy Patterson didn't live here, she knew people who did, and that meant there was always a risk of bumping into her.

I ducked into the foyer of the high-rise, which stank of bleach, and hurried over to the lifts. The one on the right was already in use. I hit the upward-pointing arrow, gingerly, because I always got static shocks off them. I'd started pressing them with a covered finger or an elbow, until Kyle caught me and wished out loud he wasn't my brother. He ignored me at school and even walked past when Roxy and her gang cut a chunk of my fringe off with scissors she'd pinched from art class. Kyle was my big brother; it was his job to look out for me, but he never did.

I counted my teeth with my tongue, waiting for the lift to arrive. Somewhere up above, it creaked into life and hurtled its way down towards the ground floor.

The back of my neck prickled. I couldn't shake the feeling Roxy was around, somewhere.

The clattering from the lift shaft continued until the twang of steel cables and a rush of air announced its arrival, groaning as it came to rest. I stepped forward, feeling the floor dip slightly under my weight. A crumpled can lay on its side, leaking an orange sticky liquid. Although it was empty, the lift smelled as if it was still full of people. I pressed the button and leaned against the handrail as the doors closed. All I had to do was make it to the seventeenth floor without the lift stopping. Heights never used to bother me when we'd moved in six years ago. Dad told me that I could be Queen of the Concrete Castle because we lived at the very top. I'd loved the fact that houses and cars looked like small toys from our windows. Aiva, Fadumo, Effi, Liam and Brooklyn all lived on the same landing as me, so there had been loads of friends to play with. Some days we'd go down to the park and build dens in the bushes or kick a football about. If we were feeling like an adventure, we'd explore the allotments and pinch ripe tomatoes and pop sweet peas into our mouths. If it was raining, we'd split into teams and race each other in the lifts until we were shouted at. And if we wanted a bigger rush than the Smiler at Alton Towers, we'd go to the roof. The door was padlocked, but there was a security camera, and Liam would wiggle his bum at it to get the concierge to chase us. Then we'd scarper in different directions, shrieking at the tops of our lungs. But one by one, Roxy had threatened my friends, scaring them off, and now it was only Jeannie who would speak to me.

As I reached the tenth floor, the cables juddered as the lift ground to a halt. The doors clattered open and there, right in front of me, stood Roxy Patterson.

I dived forward, jabbing the buttons. The doors began to close and two hands shot through the gap, wrenching them open. My foot knocked the can, which sprayed juice everywhere. The handrail dug into my back as I flattened myself against it. We glared at each other for a moment.

Roxy punched the ground-floor button on the panel and leaned back, examining one of her nails, which had broken.

My stomach plummeted faster than the lift.

Roxy had eyes the size of blackheads, daffodil-yellow hair and was built like a shed. She had a red mark on her jaw where I'd caught her with my foot. Her perfume was sweet and sickly, and her chest wheezy because of asthma.

"Don't run from me again or else." Roxy brought out an inhaler and puffed on it.

I wobbled as though we were hurtling through space rather than down a lift shaft. "Or else ... what?" I said.

"You'll find out soon enough." A smile played on her lips, which made me nervous. I much preferred it when Roxy was chasing me because it was straightforward – all I had to do was try to get away from her.

The cables twanged and the lift let out a tortured

groan. The doors gasped as they opened on the ground floor.

"This is for kicking me in the face." Roxy raised her hand. I covered my head with my arms and slid down the wall to make myself smaller.

"I wouldn't, if I were you."

A lady with Black Jack hair and Milkybar-white roots was standing there. Everyone knew Seraphina – she was the spirit medium who lived at number 111 on the fifteenth floor. Mum told me that her name was actually *Janice* and she just called herself *Seraphina* to sound mysterious. Mum also muttered her talents lay more in the drinking of spirits rather than in the talking to them.

"Why? You and some ghosts going to come and get me?" The medium said nothing. "Nah. Didn't think so." She booted one of Seraphina's shopping bags. An orange flew out and rolled across the floor. Roxy dribbled it over to the doors and then stamped on it: juice and pulp splattered everywhere. She raised her arms in the air, as though celebrating scoring a goal. "Tell anyone else my mum's a thief and you'll wish you were dead."

Seraphina looked at her. "I don't do readings for free. Your mother owes me."

"You don't need money. You're loaded."

"You can tell her I'll be round for my payment tomorrow."

"Everyone knows you're a fake." Roxy burst through the doors and out of view. I heard her shouting over to the kids in the car park.

Seraphina picked up the squashed orange and put it in the bin. She gathered up the rest of her shopping – a pack of custard creams, a can of hairspray and a dented tin of tomato soup.

I held the lift doors open for her.

"You all right?" asked Seraphina, walking into the lift.

My mouth was dry. "Couldn't be better."

Seraphina pressed the number fifteen button, which didn't light up. It was hard to tell what age she was – somewhere between thirty and one hundred. She was wearing a black leather biker jacket over a T-shirt that said *Let's Dance* and silver hoops in her ears. She reached into her handbag and scrabbled around inside it. "That one's got more hot air inside her than the Sahara Desert. Come to think of it, so does her mother." She pulled out a packet of toffees and offered me one. "They're bad for fillings, but good for morale. Nice trainers, by the way."

"My name's Ollo but you probably already know that." I released the toffee from its shiny wrapper and popped it into my mouth. "Being psychic and everything."

"Actually, I didn't. Pleased to meet you. I'm Seraphina."

"My mum says you drink spirits, is that true?" I asked with difficulty. The toffee was cementing my teeth together. "How do you drink a ghost?"

Seraphina coughed. Just as I was wondering if I should thump her on the back, she laughed. "I'll be sure to let you know if I ever manage to catch one."

I swallowed the last of my toffee and smiled.

"When you are good and ready, you'll stand up to Roxy Patterson."

"*Did dead spirits tell you that?*" I asked, my eyes as wide as two Big Ones from Dominos.

"No, it's just a hunch," she replied with a shrug.

The lift slowed down as we reached Seraphina's

floor. She stooped to pick up her shopping bags, caught sight of herself in the mirror and patted her hair. The doors opened, but she hesitated. She wore a ring with a large red stone on her pinkie, and she waved it around in front of my face.

"I don't make a habit of doing this, but my spirit guides seem to think this is important and won't shut up. That gets on my nerves because it's like having a constant whining noise in my ear. Are you ready to hear the message?"

I nodded, too startled to speak.

"They say, 'You are *never* to give in to temptation or there will be terrible consqeuences.' Does that make sense?" Her lipstick was the same colour as the brambles birds peck at in the allotments.

I didn't have the faintest clue what she was going on about.

Seraphina grabbed her bags and the lift rose slightly as she stepped out of it.

"I work in Little Whispers Café. You're welcome any time," she said over her shoulder.

The doors closed before I could say another word, and the lift continued on to the top floor.

Seraphina had to be one of the strangest people I'd ever met. Had she *really* spoken to spirit guides? And if so, what did it mean – "You are *never* to give in to temptation or there will be terrible consequences"? I glanced in the scratched mirror. There were dark circles under my eyes, my fringe was squint thanks to Roxy and my hair stuck out all over the place.

Whether Seraphina was able to speak to the dead or not, at least she'd stood up to Roxy for me. I brought my phone out of my rucksack to see I'd five missed calls from Mum. When the doors opened on my floor, I sped down the corridor. Flying into the flat, I kicked my shoes off and dumped my coat and rucksack in the hallway.

The kitchen windows were steamed up.

"Where've you been?" Kyle's cheeks bulged as he spoke with his mouth full.

"Staying as far away from you as possible." I removed a pile of mail from my seat, stuck the brown envelopes on the kitchen counter and sat at the table.

"Ollo, lose the attitude, for once." Mum's chair scraped on the floor as she stood and grabbed a dishcloth to fetch my plate, her fringe fanning up as she opened the oven door. "The point of having a phone is that you answer it when you hear a ringing noise because it means someone is wanting to speak to you. I've too much going on without having to worry about where you are. Ignore me the next time I call, and I'm not paying the credit for that phone."

"If there's no credit, you won't be able to reach me either because the phone won't work," I said, frowning.

"Keep this up and all I'll have to do is shout through the door if I want to speak to you because you'll be grounded." Mum glared at me as she placed my dinner on the table and whipped the dish towel over her shoulder.

Dad's moustache drooped at the ends, making him appear sad. When he caught me staring, he gave me a half-smile. It wasn't like him to be so quiet at dinner.

The fish fingers were burned around the edges, the baked beans had a skin over them and the mash was instant potato. At least it wasn't frankfurters again. Jeannie told me they were made from all the bits of animals that nobody wanted to eat, like snouts, ears and tails.

"Ollo? Are you listening to me?" Mum sat down again.

"I'm sorry. I was with friends and lost track of time," I said, thinking about Mr Curley, Sausage and the Dream Store.

"You don't have any friends." Kyle picked up the ketchup bottle and smacked the bottom of it, spattering sauce over his skyscraper of mash.

I got up and rifled around the cupboard for squash, but Kyle had finished the last of it. I filled a glass with water and returned to the table.

Knives and forks squeaked against plates and Kyle sniffed every two minutes. I swallowed a mouthful of powdery potato.

Kyle licked baked bean sauce off his knife. "Can I get a top for football?"

"You just got one," said Dad.

"That was their strip from three seasons ago. Everyone has their latest one." Kyle took a gulp of juice.

Mum pushed a plate of half-eaten food away from her. "We can't afford it at the moment. Maybe for your birthday?"

"That's ages away!" he said. "I never get anything."

"You just got a laptop," I pointed out as I bit into a fish finger.

Kyle's face screwed up. "It's second-hand and it's for my homework."

"You only use it for gaming and to watch skateboarding competitions on YouTube, which is a joke because you've no idea how to do a Frightmare Flip or a Ghetto Bird. The move you're best at is falling over on your backside," I said.

"Ollo!" said Mum.

"At least I have friends to go skateboarding with," he answered.

"So do I!" My face flushed the same colour as Red Kola.

"Nobody likes you."

"Take that *back*."

"Make me."

"That's enough, Kyle!" bellowed Dad.

Mum slid her hand over the top of Dad's, squeezed it and let go. She gathered up their dishes and scraped the food scraps into the recycling bin with so much vigour, it was a miracle the polka-dot pattern stayed on the plates. She banged a cupboard door shut and leaned against the kitchen top, pinching the bridge of her nose.

"There's something both of you should know," she said.

Dad began to say something but she gave him a look and he fell silent.

"We all want new things. I could do with a washing machine so I don't have to spend every weekend in the launderette watching your clothes going round in circles. But it's not going to happen because Dad lost his job today and we've got mouths to feed, rent to pay and the bills are stacking up. No matter how much we all think we need something, we can't afford it at the moment."

Kyle and I stared at Dad.

"What happened?" I whispered.

Dad slammed his fists on the table, making us all jump. "I'm being replaced in the warehouse by *machinery*. I'm supposed to be the head of this family – and your mum's talking about going to the food bank to feed us. A *food bank!*"

I tried to picture what a bank that only gave out food looked like.

"It'll only be until we get back on our feet." Mum put her hand on his shoulder. He shrugged it off.

"I can't get my son a new football shirt, my daughter some drops so she can have her first dream, my wife a washing machine or take my family away on holiday. I can't even put food on the table. Do you know how that makes me feel?" Dad's voice splintered like peanut brittle.

Mum sat beside him, rubbed his back and rested her head against his. Seeing Dad this upset made my hunger vanish.

All of us sat in silence for a minute. Then Kyle leapt up, grabbed his phone and mumbled that he'd be back later.

I got up too. I wasn't used to seeing Dad like this. He was the one who always had a grin on his face or something cheerful to say if you'd had a rubbish day at school. I knew exactly what it felt like when someone didn't want you around because they'd made their mind up you weren't good enough.

“Dad,” I said. “Machines aren’t kind and they’ll never make people laugh like you do.”

He gave me a tight-lipped smile. I shut the kitchen door behind me and headed to my room.

The moon pressed its silvery face against the window and the stars sat in the sky like thousands of white stone chips set in black tarmac. I closed the curtains and changed into my pyjamas, then climbed into bed and curled up like a hedgehog. My arms and legs ached from scrambling over walls away from Roxy.

I glanced at the picture stuck to my mirror of me and Jeannie laughing together. Whatever plan Roxy was hatching, at least I had Jeannie.

My mind drifted off to the Dream Store, with its shelves packed with gleaming bottles filled with the promise of magic and adventure. I wiggled my toes – even the smell of the place was exciting. I would love to see Mr Curley and Sausage again. I remembered the note with the assistant’s job that had fallen from the wall, the beautiful writing on the card.

I blinked and sat bolt upright in bed.

What if I applied for the assistant's job? I didn't have any experience, but it was worth a shot. If I got the job, I'd be able to save my wages, so I could buy the drops. Then I could finally have the dream I'd always longed for *and* help Mum and Dad with the bills.

My heart raced around the insides of my ribs and as I settled back down in bed, my happy sighs made all the empty dream catchers above me flutter.

CHAPTER 3

The river rushed along, slapping the banks and polishing stones. A hunched heron crouched on a rusted shopping trolley, pretending he wasn't there. The sun pushed its way through the trees, throwing the reflections of leaves across my path that bowed and shook like shadow puppets.

After checking for any signs of Roxy Patterson, I scanned the park for Jeannie. She lived in a different block of flats from me, but if it wasn't raining, we'd always meet up and walk to school together.

I'd know that electric-blue hoodie and those

emoji-heart-red trainers anywhere. She was waiting for me on our favourite bench. I sped up, vaulting over puddles and sidestepping an empty dog poo bag that swirled around in circles in the breeze. I threw myself down beside Jeannie, startling her.

"What did you do that for?" she said, pulling her jacket around her.

"Eh, it's me, not Kylo Ren."

"So you managed to escape from Roxy yesterday?" she said, looking the other way while she spun a ring, with a green plastic spider on it, around her finger.

"I'm alive, aren't I?"

Jeannie turned, sniffed, and gave me a forced smile. That's when I noticed she'd four scratches across her cheek as if she'd been clawed by a feral cat. Her eyes were watery and the tip of her nose bright pink.

"What happened to you?"

Jeannie slid down the bench, so her head was resting against the back of it. She fixed her eyes on the river. "Roxy Patterson. She said she'd do worse if you run from her again."

I gasped. So that's what Roxy had been hinting at in the lift. If I fled from Roxy and her gang, they'd turn on Jeannie. The last friend I had. I couldn't stand the thought of Roxy harming her because of me. My fists clenched, turning my fingers the same colour as the bones underneath my skin. "I'm going to Mrs Stanton about her."

"No way. You know what happened to Kelli McLean when she told on her. Got so bad she had to leave. Kelli said even at her new school she's still scared Roxy's going to come for her."

I puffed the longest part of my fringe out of my eyes. "We'll just steer clear of her then."

"That'll maybe work for a day or two, not for the rest of the year." Jeannie sighed. "Ollo, I'm not as fast as you; she's always going to catch up with me." She sat up and faced me. "If we don't see each other for a while, Roxy Patterson will forget that we even exist and then she'll find some other losers to pick on."

"As plans go, that one sucks." I folded my arms.

"My gran's already in hospital with a broken hip – I don't want to wind up in the bed next to her because of Roxy." Jeannie checked her phone and stood, throwing her bag on to her shoulder, which made her ponytail swish to the side. "It's just until things calm down. I'd better get going otherwise I'm going to be late."

"You don't even want us to walk to school together?"

Jeannie pulled out a strawberry lace from her bag, which she ripped in half, handing me a piece. She knew they were my very favourite. "I'll see you later – well, you know what I mean." Jeannie scurried off towards the bridge and gave me a quick wave before she disappeared over it.

I shoved the strawberry lace into my pocket and walked along kicking stones off the path. My stomach hurt as though it was filled with splinters, volcanic lava, coils of barbed wire and stinging wasps.

This was the worst day of my life.

Without Jeannie I had no one. I stomped over the bridge, pausing at the highest point to peer over the side of it. The trees rippling on the surface of the water below were exactly the same colour as the bottles of Safari Adventure DreamDrops. I thought about the card in the Dream Store, fluttering down from the wall and landing at my feet. I was more determined than ever to apply for that job. Because if I could afford to dream, then Roxy would have to leave me alone – and Jeannie and I could be friends again.

I spent most of the day creeping around the school corridors and had even hidden in the supply cupboard on the third floor to avoid Roxy. I'd packed up my bag before the end of the class and left as soon as the final bell had rung.

I raced out of school, along the road and down the steps, avoiding the wobbly paving stones at the bottom. I sped along, keeping my head down, until I finally swerved into Hidden Lane, my belly wriggling with nerves. I stopped for a moment and took some deep breaths. I checked my reflection in the window of the Dream Store. My face was as pale as flour and my hair was a mess. I smoothed it down and pinched my cheeks.

The bell tinkled as I went inside. The aroma of

hot cinnamon apple pie filled the shop, a smell so delicious I closed my eyes to breathe in deep. When I opened them, Mr Curley was standing in front of me with Sausage perched on his shoulder.

"Ollo? Has something happened?" He looked out the window. "Are the marauding girls bothering you again?"

I frantically thought back to the requirements for the job. *Must have a vivid imagination. Warm smile preferable.*

I smiled, showing as many of my teeth as possible.

Mr Curley stood, puzzled. "Are you hurt?"

I lost the smile. "No, Mr Curley; I'm here about the job." He was silent and I pointed nervously to the card pinned on the wall. "The assistant's job."

"Knickers," cackled Sausage.

"Language, Sausage!" Mr Curley glanced at the notice and then at me. The corners of his mouth twitched as though he found something amusing.

I tapped my foot, making the tile underneath it flash white. "I could start right away," I added.

"Oh. You were being serious!" Mr Curley brought

his hand up to his mouth, in order to hide his smile behind it.

I nodded.

"Ollo, the post is for a grown-up," he said gently. "It's just Sausage and me manning the fort. We ideally need someone who has a few years of customer experience under their belt."

I stuck my chin out. "I can be nice to strangers, even if they're really annoying."

"The role requires a certain understanding of chemistry, physics and engineering," Mr Curley went on. "I didn't put that on the notice because it's more important the candidate is a good fit with the store. It's not just any old business we're running here."

I swallowed. I could feel the chance of having a dream slipping away. Jeannie would never be my friend again and Roxy Patterson would make my life a misery ... *for ever.*

"I'm not allergic to feathers, Mr Curley." To my embarrassment, my eyes filled up with tears.

Mr Curley shook his head. "I've upset you, haven't I?"

I've been so stupid, I thought. *Of course Mr Curley will never consider me.*

The tile lit up under my foot as I pivoted on the spot and headed for the door.

Sausage flapped her wings. *"Put the kettle on!"* she croaked.

I left the Dream Store. The cobbles blended into one long grey smudge as I fled down Hidden Lane.

"Ollo!"

I halted, my heart booming in my ears. I turned.

Mr Curley stood outside the Dream Store, waving. "Why don't we have a chat about the job over a cuppa, shall we?"

I hesitated for a second before I walked back towards to the Dream Store. Sausage did a loop the loop in the air after me, trumpeting at the top of her lungs.

CHAPTER 4

I'd never had an interview for a job before. I wiped the tips of my trainers on the backs of my legs and straightened my skirt before I went into the shop. Following Mr Curley and Sausage through the green velvet curtains at the back of the store, I clattered down a wrought-iron spiral staircase into the basement.

Woven rugs hung from the walls, alongside oil paintings and mirrors that were squint. Shelves had warped under the weight of hundreds of books. Clocks ticked beside carved white busts which peeped out from behind flowering plants, that cascaded down over collections of pottery, arrowheads, seashells and clay pipes.

It was the kind of place where your eyes would never be bored.

"Take a seat." Mr Curley gestured to a couple of squishy sofas in the middle of the room.

I dumped my rucksack on the floor, shook off my coat and draped it over the back of the sofa. I yanked down my shirtsleeves to hide the bruises on my arms and sat, hugging a cushion with a leopard embroidered on it.

"Tea, Ollo? I have oolong, Cloud Mist Green, Golden Monkey Jin Hou or one from Papua New Guinea that promotes inner peace and a sense of *oneness* with the world?"

I hesitated. "Do you have any hot chocolate?"

"Coming right up."

"You've got more books than our school library," I said as Mr Curley busied himself filling the kettle. "Have you read anything by Jacqueline Wilson?"

"Is she an expert on dreams?" asked Mr Curley.

"Of sorts, but probably not the ones you're talking about," I answered.

"Since the dawn of time people have dreamed and we've never ceased to be fascinated by them." He brought over a tray with a mug of hot chocolate and a pot of tea. He set down milk, sugar, teaspoons and a pile of shortbread rounds.

Kyle had finished the Honey Monster Puffs this morning and Mum had to use this week's lunch money to charge the key for the electricity meter, so I was starving. I grabbed a biscuit and munched it. I shut my eyes because the taste was so buttery and delicious. I tried the hot chocolate next, which was warm and silky.

"The Naskapi hunters of Labrador track caribou in their dreams. They teach their children that dreams can provide them with food." Mr Curley offered me another biscuit and I took three. Then I remembered I was at an interview, so I snapped one of them in half and put it back.

"The Aborigines believe that our entire world and everything that exists in it was made by a dream, and the Blackfoot Indians think that when we dream it is just as real as when we are in the waking world. The Crow people would even go as far as to cut off a part of their finger in the hope of receiving great wisdom in their sleep." Mr Curley poured out the tea and sat opposite, selecting a piece of shortbread. "Dreams are the one thing that unites us all; they are quite simply magical."

This made me want one all the more. "How come the drops cost so much?"

"The ingredients used to make them are exceptionally rare, which makes them costly. But what price can you put on learning, and discovering more about yourself in a nightmare-free experience where the benefits will last you a lifetime?" replied Mr Curley.

"Five euros!" crowed Sausage.

"Sausage – any more of that and you'll go outside," Mr Curley said in a way that was clear he'd never follow through with the threat.

"You'll go outside!" Sausage mimicked Mr Curley's voice perfectly, and I laughed.

My eyes sparkled. "Are you richer than the Queen, Mr Curley?"

He thought about my question as he drained his teacup. "I think it's safe to assume she'll have more in the bank than me. All my profits are ploughed back into my work because it's my ambition to provide dreams that entertain, educate and protect children against nightmares."

"Oh," I said, stroking the leopard on the cushion. "What's in the DreamDrops?"

"Pickled herrings and sweaty socks." Sausage flapped up to the highest shelf, out of Mr Curley's reach.

"Magic," Mr Curley replied.

I glanced at him and then at Sausage, waiting to see who would dissolve into fits of laughter first, but neither of them did.

"You very nearly had me there," I said, rolling my eyes.

Mr Curley gave me a funny look.

"What do they taste of?" I asked, secretly hoping they were nothing like prawn cocktail crisps, boiled carrots, salad cream or marmalade: four of my least favourite flavours.

"This varies from person to person, but they will only ever taste of things you love. However, no matter how delicious, the bottles have a special time release mechanism that only allows one drop per evening at the set time of your choosing."

I could hardly contain my excitement. One day soon I would try the DreamDrops – but first I would need to earn the money to buy them. I polished off the last half piece of shortbread, brushed the sugar from my lips and swept the granules off my lap on to the floor. I sat up, with my head held high.

"I'm ready for my interview, Mr Curley."

He leaned back on the sofa and crossed his legs. "Tell me three things about yourself, Ollo."

Sausage's beak opened slightly as she waited to hear my answer.

My mind went blank. In a panic, my eyes roved around the room until they settled on a cracked oil painting of a poppy.

"My favourite colour is red. Kyle says it's fitting because it's a sign of danger and everyone should be warned of my presence. I try not to pay any attention to my older brother, Mr Curley, because he picks his nose every time he watches YouTube but isn't able to pick his pants up off his bedroom floor."

Mr Curley's cloud-like eyebrows drifted up his forehead.

I bit my lip, not convinced I'd impressed him enough to give me the job.

Sausage chuckled and glided down to the table, where she settled.

I thought of something better. "I'm the best runner at my school. Mrs McGarvey, my gym teacher, says I'm faster than a greyhound with a jetpack because I only ever eat strawberry laces, but that's not true because I also love Monster Munch sandwiches." I paused to clear my throat. "Mr Curley, picture the scene: you're swamped with children and there's a rush on Safari Adventure DreamDrops. The shelves are empty – but you're busy dealing with a stroppy customer and Sausage can't carry the bottles in her beak, so what are you going to do? If you hired me, *nobody* could fetch Safari Adventure DreamDrops from the storeroom faster. And if you give me a chance, I'll be sure not to smash any more bottles."

Sausage nodded at me. Two frown lines appeared between Mr Curley's eyes.

I clasped my hands together so tightly that my fingers throbbed. I had one more chance to impress Mr Curley.

Perhaps I should tell him the truth?

My shoulders lowered as I puffed a storm's worth of air out my mouth.

"You won't find anyone who knows more about the drops, Mr Curley. You bring out six new dreams a year – each one better than the last, packed with the most exciting adventures you could ever wish for. No one at school wants their boring old dreams any more, not when they can sail the seven seas looking for treasure or explore new planets in space. And best of all, they can do all this without ever having a nightmare, which I've heard can be really scary." I licked my lips. "I've wanted to come into your shop for so long . . ."

"Why didn't you?" Mr Curley asked curiously.

"It would have broken my heart leaving without the drops. I can't afford them." Roxy Patterson's taunts echoed around inside my head. I picked at a thread on the hem of my skirt until it started unravelling. "Having one of your dreams would mean so much to me, Mr Curley – more than you could ever possibly imagine. You see, there's something wrong with me. But if I got a job here and saved up my wages, I could finally take the DreamDrops and then I'd be cured. And I wouldn't be different any more: I'd be just like everyone else at school."

Mr Curley had lowered his teacup. "Whatever is the matter with you, Ollo?"

"I've never had a dream."

Mr Curley's teacup dropped from his hand, bounced off his leg and fell to the floor, where it spun under the table, his eyes wide in shock.

"Knickers," said Sausage.

This time, Mr Curley didn't ask her to mind her language. In fact, he didn't utter a word.

I'd blown my interview. *Big time.*

I had been so stupid. Of course the Dream Store wouldn't employ an assistant who couldn't dream. That would be like hiring a lifeguard who couldn't swim.

Leaping to my feet, I grabbed my coat and rucksack, tore up the staircase and burst through the curtains, just as a group of children trooped in, their faces flushed with excitement.

I pushed past them to the doorway. As I opened it, Mr Curley called my name.

"Ollo," he said. "Wait a minute."

He took down the card pinned to the wall and ripped it into tiny pieces, tossing them up in the air. "Congratulations, Ollo! You've got the job," said Mr Curley.

My mouth fell open. "Seriously?"

Sausage swooped around sounding like a thousand fireworks going off, and some of the children ducked in fright.

"Come back tomorrow after school, Ollo. Don't be late."

"Will I get double time on bank holidays and Christmas?" I asked.

"Don't push your luck, young lady," he replied.

"You won't regret this, Mr Curley, I promise." I left the Dream Store, the bell tinkling as I closed the door behind me.

My insides felt as though they were filled with shaken-up cans of cherry cola, popping candy, feather dusters and sparklers. I couldn't wipe the smile from my face.

Even though I was placing one foot in front of the other, I could have sworn I was floating along Hidden Lane.

CHAPTER 5

Seeing her always made my heart beat out of rhythm like the school band. It was home time and Roxy Patterson was perched on the wall with her gang, chucking Maltesers at people as they poured through the school gates.

I slotted myself in beside a group of older girls, keeping my head down, so Roxy wouldn't notice me. There was nothing lonelier than pretending you were friends with a bunch of strangers. I hadn't seen Jeannie all day. At lunchtime I'd walked straight into Roxy on the way to my locker, along with her goons. In the struggle, I'd knocked Roxy's phone out of her hand and the screen had cracked. She was just about to give me a fresh set of bruises when the head teacher had appeared and Roxy had no choice but to slink off.

As I neared the end of the street, I glanced over my shoulder. Thankfully, Roxy wasn't looking my way. She was talking to someone.

To Jeannie.

I blinked, not quite believing my eyes.

They were laughing.

Together.

As though they were old friends.

I froze and the girls who were shielding me walked on.

Roxy Patterson spotted me and leapt off the wall, yelling for her gang. Jeannie stayed put.

I dashed down the steps, willing my legs to move faster. Double-decker buses roared past me, sounding the same as TIE fighters from Star Wars. I narrowly avoided a man weaving his way out of the Storm Queen pub. I fled around the corner into Hidden Lane, relieved there was no traffic warden to collide with. I sprinted over the smooth cobbles to the Dream Store, then I darted inside, slamming the door behind me.

A blur of girls stampeded past like a pack of baying hounds after a fox.

I let out a sigh of relief, wiped the sweat from my brow and looked around the store. It was busy. Trainers squeaked as children ran over the floor, making the square tiles flash. Friends laughed and chattered as they picked up the bottles, showing each other the adventures they wanted. The air crackled with excitement.

Without warning, the walls and floor dimmed to black. The kids whistled as though they knew what was going to happen. A fanfare sounded and everyone shuffled towards the empty space at the back of the room, leaving the middle of the floor clear. I moved over to the wall, wondering what was going on.

The tiles on the floor beneath us changed into screens that began playing footage of long, rippling blades of grass. Gnarled trees lined three of the walls, as though we were standing in ancient woods. The whole store echoed with the noises of owls hooting, trees sighing and a wolf howling in the distance. A girl next to me gasped and pointed. I followed her finger up to the ceiling, which had transformed into a night sky, crammed with twinkling stars. The moon wore a skirt of frothy clouds. My nose filled with the fresh scent of pine cones, leaves and damp earth. The trees beside me began to part, sending shards of twigs and leaves flying. Something large grunted from the depths of its belly. I glanced around, the hairs on my neck standing on end. The young girl beside me was grinning. I willed my legs to stop trembling.

I caught my breath as a long snout covered in green scales pushed through the branches. And then a dragon barrelled into the clearing in front of us.

I flattened myself against the wall. The huge creature let out a deafening snort and turned in a circle, flicking its long tail. Trails of smoke leaked from its nostrils, and its eyes glowed traffic-light red.

Sweat trickled down my back. I hadn't felt fear like this since being chased by Roxy and her gang.

There was a whinnying noise to the left of us,

and then a black horse sailed over a fallen tree trunk. Its hooves thundered as it landed and skidded to a halt in the clearing, its flanks sheened with sweat. Astride it was a boy knight, whose armour flashed shooting-star silver when the horse reared up and kicked out its front legs.

The knight dismounted and faced the dragon, who edged away from him. The boy drew not one but two swords and approached in measured steps, his armour clanking.

"You'll never beat me, foe of mine!" he spat. The knight's horse showed its teeth, snorted and shook its mane.

There was a blood-curdling roar from the dragon. It opened its mouth and blasted the boy with a jet of neon-yellow flames. Raising his swords, the knight spun them around so fast, they extinguished the fire, turning it to smoke. The dragon lashed out with its tail, which the knight cleared in one leap. In a flourish, the boy twirled his swords and then launched them through the air. They struck the branch directly above the dragon's head. As the creature stretched its wings to take off, there was a loud crack. The branch fell, smacking the beast on the head. The dragon wobbled and collapsed into a heap with a groan. Triumphant, the knight pulled his swords from the branch, rotated them around his head and put them away in his scabbards. He pointed at the children in the crowd. "In A Knight's Adventure, I'll show you and you and you all these moves and more, so that you too can become a legend and conquer dragons in your dreams. Terms and conditions apply." The boy knight bowed to the audience, who exploded into whoops and applause.

I couldn't take my eyes off him. I'd never seen anyone so fearless or strong in my life.

As the knight strode by, I reached out, wanting to tell him how amazing he'd been.

My hand passed straight though him.

He wasn't real.

The bright lights returned and the knight, his horse, the woods and the dragon vanished.

Another fanfare sounded and a flag appeared on the wall emblazoned with the words: *A Knight's Adventure DreamDrops. Be your own hero tonight. Available while stocks last.*

That's when it dawned on me.

If I bought this dream, the knight could show me some killer moves. And if I was able to defend myself against a dragon, fighting Roxy Patterson would be a piece of cake. I really could be my own hero.

Queues began to form all the way up to the mezzanine as children hurried to buy bottles of A Knight's Adventure from the self-service checkouts. I pushed my way through the green velvet curtains. I bolted down the stairs, jumping off the last one. The sooner I could start work, the faster I could save up for the drops. The scent of freshly baked scones and warm butter filled the room. Mr Curley and Sausage must be around somewhere.

"Hello? Mr Curley? Sausage?"

There were some boxes sitting on the table. One of them was labelled *A Knight's Adventure.* Mr Curley had told me to stay away from the drops – probably because he was worried I might damage something again. But I was curious. I pulled out a bottle with a silver knight's helmet for a stopper. The raised outlines of flying dragons and swords were all over the smoky-grey glass. When I pressed the top of the bottle, I heard a bugle and steel swords clashing.

Gazing at it with longing, I held the bottle to the light, but the glass was too dark for me to peer through. I wondered if the drops fizzed on your tongue or if they were more like kola cubes and took ages to finish. It was agonizing. All that stood between me and a Roxy Patterson–free life was a thin layer of glass.

"There you are, Ollo!" Mr Curley appeared with Sausage perched on his shoulder.

I whipped the bottle behind my back.

"Naughty! Naughty!" crowed Sausage. *"Very naughty!"*

I flushed the same colour as Strawberry Crush Hubba Bubba as I dropped the bottle back in its box.

"Did you have a good day at school?" asked Mr Curley.

"Fantastic," I lied.

Mr Curley brought over a tray which had a plate piled high with scones and pots of raspberry jam and butter.

My stomach let out a loud rumble.

"Would you care for one?" asked Mr Curley, passing me the plate.

"I thought you'd never ask, Mr Curley." I grabbed a scone, slathered it in butter and dolloped on so much jam, it oozed over the sides. Steam rose from my mug of hot chocolate, which Mr Curley had filled to the brim.

There was a flurry of feathers and Sausage landed on the table, skidding to a halt. Her head bobbed up and down as she watched me eating. I broke a piece of the scone off and gave it to her.

"Now you see it," croaked the bird. She tipped her head back and swallowed it in one go. *"Now it's s'cone."*

I laughed. "Am I being paid to eat, Mr Curley?"

"Today, you are." He stirred his tea with the handle of a butter knife as he put his feet up on the table. The soles of his shoes had holes in them.

"Did you enjoy the advert for A Knight's Adventure?" he asked.

"It was the best thing I've ever seen in my whole life, Mr Curley. I know the dragon and the knight weren't real, but they sort of were. How did you do that?" I licked some jam off my finger.

"A mixture of holograms, projections, scents and sound effects. If you can give children a flavour of the dream, it makes them keen to try it out."

"Well, it worked for me, Mr Curley." I helped myself to another scone, just to check it tasted as good as the first one. "I loved it so much, I want A Knight's Adventure to be my very first dream – once I've saved up my wages."

Mr Curley's face became very serious. Sausage gave a long, slow whistle and took off from the table to sit on the bookcase.

"Ollo, there's something I have to tell you and there's no easy way for me to say it."

Sausage hid her head under her wing.

I stuck my tongue out the side of my mouth, fishing for crumbs.

"You can never take the DreamDrops." His eyes were dark blue now, like deep pools.

"Why not?" I asked.

"If you've never had a dream before, the interaction between the drops and your subconscious is too dangerous. The drops become unstable and can conjure up a nightmare so bad that your life, as well as that of many others, would be in danger."

I swallowed. "Couldn't I just try half a drop?" I begged. "A nibble of one?"

Sausage flew down from her perch and settled next to me on the sofa. She opened her beak and plopped a Brazil nut into my lap.

Two fat tears rolled down my cheeks. Mr Curley knelt by my side and gave me his handkerchief. I blew my nose, folded it and blew my nose again. The handkerchief was full and squishy, so I gave it back to Mr Curley, who took it gingerly between his thumb and forefinger and placed it on the table.

"It's my job to protect children, not to put them in harm's way. If anything happened to you, I'd never forgive myself, and that's why I must ask you never to take the drops."

"Why did you give me the job if you knew I could never have a dream?"

Mr Curley stood and went to the sink, where he filled a glass of water. He handed it to me. "Because what you believe to be a terrible flaw is actually a gift."

I scowled. I couldn't imagine how. The only gift it

had brought me was the attention of the school bully. Mr Curley sat opposite me. "Ollo, there is something quite extraordinary about you."

My eyes slid over to Sausage, expecting the bird to cackle. She looked at me with her head on one side.

"Because you can't dream at night and can only dream by day, this has made your imagination way more powerful than anyone else's."

"Kyle says I'm good at telling tales," I said.

Mr Curley smiled. "Imagination is one of the most important skills we can possess. Look at everything around us: the chairs, the kettle, the cutlery, the cups, the lights – these are all things someone somewhere had the idea to create. Like life-saving medicines, the internet, and space exploration. Not only can our imaginations help us solve everyday problems, they're the key to smarter thinking, which is how we make our world a better place to live in."

I drank some water, wondering who'd invented glasses.

"Should you still wish to work at the Dream Store, I'll show you how to use your gift, but I can only do this on the understanding you will *never* take the drops. If you no longer want to be employed here because of this, then I'd understand and would let you go with the sum of two months' wages for your troubles."

I fixed my gaze on a stuffed fox in a case that was baring its teeth. I still couldn't get my head around never being able to have a dream. And to be surrounded by DreamDrops knowing I could not take them made it worse.

"Can I go home now?" I said.

Mr Curley got to his feet. "Of course, Ollo."

I fetched my coat and rucksack and climbed the spiral stairs as if I was scaling a wrought-iron mountain. I pushed my way through the velvet curtains to see children tearing around the shop, shrieking with glee as they busied themselves selecting the dreams they coveted.

The bell tinkled as Mr Curley opened the door for me. He stared at me in a way that told me my answer was really important to him. "Will we see you tomorrow, Ollo?" he said. I paused. Sausage settled on his shoulder and stuck her head forward to hear my reply.

I shrugged and nodded.

Mr Curley's eyes crinkled at the sides and Sausage let out a toot like a party blower.

It was impossible to smile back at them. I walked to the top of the lane in a daze and drifted past the shops like a leaf in a river.

I couldn't pack the job in, not when Mum and Dad were relying on me for some extra money.

"*Hey! Ollo!* Wait up," shouted a voice.

I turned to see Seraphina locking the door of Little Whispers Café and hurrying to catch up with me. She had on a *Choose Life* T-shirt under her leather jacket, which was strange because it was her job to speak to the dead.

"I need to talk to you," she said, striding alongside me. "My spirit guides won't let it lie. They want to make sure you know that you are to stay away from temptation, do you hear? Or else there will be dire consequences." She glanced at me. "Does that mean anything to you?"

"I ate seven strawberry laces at lunchtime, if that's what they're on about," I said, gloomily.

She snorted. "Oh, that's nothing. I devoured three slabs of red velvet cake. I had a bad reading."

"What happened?" I asked.

"I finally connected a husband and wife. He told her that he preferred it in heaven because he wasn't kept awake by her snoring. The woman refused to pay me and slammed the café door on her way out, which made my crystal ball roll off a shelf and smash on the floor. I'm hoping it's not a bad omen."

Before I could say a word, there was a commotion across the street. Roxy Patterson and her gang were there, shouting names at me at the tops of their voices. The crowd at the bus stop gawped as though they were watching a soap on TV.

I had no fight left in me now that Mr Curley told me I couldn't have a dream.

Seraphina yelled back at them. "If you don't leave her alone, I'm going to put a wart hex on you, Roxy Patterson, and let's face it, you need all the help you can get, love. So, jog on."

Roxy screamed something at us that made an old lady's dog bark and then she kicked over the sign outside the bakers.

"Can you really do a wart hex?" I asked, grateful that Seraphina had stuck up for me, again.

"I'm a healer as well as a medium, so I'm more likely to cure you of them – but she doesn't know that." Seraphina hooked her arm through mine. "Ollo, pay no attention to those idiots. It's not being different you should worry about; it's being exactly the same as them. Anyway, who wants to be just like everyone else?" Seraphina made a bleating noise like a sheep as we took the steps down to the underpass.

Whatever age she was, Seraphina didn't act it.

CHAPTER 6

"Are you all right, Ollo?" said Mr Curley. "You look like you've had a shock."

"I'm fine," I said.

"Oh, no, you're not!" cried Sausage from Mr Curley's shoulder.

Sausage was right and so was Mr Curley.

I'd thrown myself into my job at the Dream Store. Even though I was still being picked on by Roxy, spending time with Mr Curley and Sausage gave me something to look forward to. I loved stocking the shelves, carefully, with the beautiful bottles, and watching the children's faces when a new advert for the DreamDrops played out on the shop floor. After I had been there for three months, Mr Curley even let me help with the customers because he said I was a natural at matching children with their perfect dream. Only when the store was quiet would I gaze longingly at the A Knight's Adventure bottles, wishing I could try the DreamDrops and learn how to outsmart Roxy.

Today, after the school bell had gone, Roxy Patterson spotted me at the gates. She whooped and called for her gang. I'd run faster than the wind to Hidden Lane, not looking behind me once, and ducked into the Dream Store. When the girls had sprinted past the window, I saw that Jeannie was with them too.

"Mr Curley, why can't I dream?" My voice shook with anger. "Everyone else can."

He studied me for a while before nodding. "I was wondering when you'd ask me this and I think you're ready for the truth, Ollo." He bolted the door and flipped the open sign to closed.

I followed him to the basement, where I took a seat.

Sausage fluttered around from the sofa to the shelves and then on to the head of the statue, unable to settle.

Mr Curley drummed his fingers on his knees. "First of all, I need to tell you something about myself. I am the owner of the Dream Store, but it's not my only job. I am also Tannis Curley: Guardian of Dreamers."

I didn't move a muscle. I didn't even blink.

"Being a Guardian of Dreamers means it's my responsibility to ensure children have good dreams." He paused. "You're not believing a word of this, are you?"

"It's a bit like me telling you I'm Wonder Woman, Mr Curley."

"I take your point. I think there's something you should see. Sausage, can you open the door?"

There was a painting of a wolfhound on the wall. Sausage flew to it and tapped the dog's nose four times with her beak. A large Persian rug on the wall moved to the side to reveal a hidden door.

"Come," said Mr Curley, entering the room.

It was empty, except for a lit glass case that was

twice my height. Inside it, sitting on a lectern, was a book that looked very old. The pages were cream and edged with gold, which glowed under the spotlight.

"Did you know every twenty-four hours there are thirty-five billion dreams in the world?" said Mr Curley, his voice quiet as he continued to stare at it.

My skin tingled. As I gazed at the book, words appeared on the page, as though being written by an invisible hand. When the words neared the bottom of the page, it turned over.

"Is this another light projection like the knight and dragon, Mr Curley?"

"No, Ollo. This is the Book of Dreams and it records every good dream a child has in the world, taking note of the date and time. They make for quite the most wonderful reading."

I watched, hypnotized, as the pages filled up. Pressing my nose against the glass, I read about children who changed into mermaids in the rain, zoomed around the world on clouds and made wishes come true when they sneezed.

"Why are they being written down?" I said.

"Every time a child dreams, good energy is

released into the air, making the world a happier, more harmonious place. Each one is recorded so I can monitor their numbers: the more there are, the better it is for our planet." Mr Curley frowned. "However, just as dreams exist, so must nightmares. These two opposing forces are inseparable and have coexisted together since the beginning of time."

"If you're the Guardian of Dreamers then who's in charge of the nightmares?" I held my breath.

"Her name is Myrdina and she's the Mother of All Nightmares. I doubt there's ever been such a wicked soul responsible for bad dreams."

Goosebumps rose on my arms.

"Does she have a shop too? Because the lady who works in Sweet Treats Candy Store is really rude to children," I whispered.

"Perish the thought, Ollo. Myrdina is only supposed to exist in the dream world because scaring children when they're awake is strictly forbidden by the Guild of Dreamers and Nightmares."

"Who are they?"

"They are all the Guardians of Dreamers and Mothers of All Nightmares who existed before

Myrdina and myself. They keep the harmony between this world and the dream one."

I paused, taking in everything he had said. "Has something happened, Mr Curley?"

"Come with me," he said.

I took one last look at the Book of Dreams and we left the room. Sausage flew up to the painting and pecked at it. The door closed.

Mr Curley led me over to another wall of the basement, where an impressive gilt mirror was hanging.

"If you'd do the honours once again, Sausage."

The bird shook herself and glided towards a candlestick holder jutting out from the wall. Sausage landed on it, flapping her wings until it had tilted at right angles to the side.

The mirror in front of us slid aside to reveal a small room. In the middle of the floor was a large square structure built from bricks.

I glanced at Mr Curley. He looked stern. A sense of dread washed over me. Mr Curley carefully removed four of the bricks, revealing a thick panel of glass behind them.

"Take a look, Ollo," he said.

I walked up to the window and stood on my tiptoes.

Sitting on top of a slab of concrete was a large black leather-bound book. Its cover bulged and rippled, as though something was alive inside it.

"This is the Book of Nightmares, Ollo," said Mr Curley. "It records every bad dream that children have in the world."

The book cracked open, making me jump. I could hear children screaming. Words appeared as though scratched on to the page, some of them cutting the paper. I leaned in as close as I dared and read about shadows that became monsters, sandwiches that ate kids and red-eyed dolls with wings. The book slammed itself shut, a dark liquid oozing from its pages. I watched as the Book of Nightmares tilted upwards, angling itself in my direction, as if aware of my presence. For a split second I could have sworn I saw the shape of a face under the cover. I backed away and quickly replaced the bricks.

Mr Curley had moved to stand beside a box with

a blind covering the top of it. He nodded at me and I pulled it up to discover a black mask inside.

"What's *this*?" I said.

"It belongs to Myrdina," replied Mr Curley. "For a long time, she was excellent at her job and, as required, only scared a small number of children every night. But Myrdina slowly began to develop a taste for it and became greedy. The more children she terrorized, the stronger she became. Twenty years ago, she started to frighten so many kids, the Book of Dreams ceased recording good dreams and the Book of Nightmares filled with bad ones. The skies here changed: storms raged, the earth trembled and fires blazed out of control. Eventually Myrdina became so powerful, she was able to escape from the dream world into our world."

A real, living nightmare wandering around Parradicehill.

"When she was here, the Mother of All Nightmares frightened children the whole time, not just when they were dreaming. Some of the poor souls were so petrified they turned to stone."

I gasped.

The mask in the case twitched and I watched, astounded, as its mouth widened into a grin. I was glad when Mr Curley pulled the blind down.

"It was agreed by the Guild that she had broken the rules and should be punished. They decided she must go back to the dream world, but that she should continue with her work. I made a magic essence that imprisoned her there. Myrdina still creates bad dreams, but because I confiscated the Book of Nightmares I can monitor her activity closely. The mask is an extra insurance policy. Without it, she can never survive in this world."

I thought about what he'd said for a minute or two, churning it all over in my mind.

"That's why you invented DreamDrops, isn't it, Mr Curley? So there'd never be too many nightmares again."

Mr Curley nodded. "That is correct, Ollo. The drops make sure the balance between dreams and nightmares has once again been restored."

More children's cries came from the Book of Nightmares and a shiver travelled the length of my body.

I scooted out the room without so much as a backwards glance.

Sausage trumpeted as we reappeared and pushed the candlestick so it sat straight again. The mirror closed and Mr Curley checked it was secure.

"Why are you showing me all this, Mr Curley?" I asked. "What does it have to do with me not being able to dream?"

Sausage settled on a bookshelf, watching.

Mr Curley looked as though the Book of Nightmares had sucked the life from him. He sat on the sofa and smiled at me. "Ollo, you too are a Guardian of Dreamers. This is why you are not meant to dream. Your imagination is so vivid that what you dream of will come to life. You could unwittingly bring Myrdina back into this world."

My mouth opened and then shut again.

"I understand it's a lot to take in, Ollo. You're bound to feel overwhelmed with everything you've learned today."

"How do you know I am a Guardian of Dreamers?"

"I didn't until you mentioned you couldn't

dream. It's an exceptionally rare trait shared by all Guardians"

"How many of them are there?" I said, my eyes wide.

"Not including Guild members, there are perhaps ten others in the world at present. Every sixty years the old Guardian must be replaced by a new one, specially chosen by the Guild. Unfortunately, not everyone who is a Guardian will have the qualities it takes for such an extraordinary and privileged role."

I couldn't share Mr Curley's enthusiasm. None of this solved the problem of Roxy Patterson or how I was going to be best friends with Jeannie again. And worst of all, I'd never be able to have a dream.

As though he was reading my mind, Mr Curley led me towards the stairs. "I know this feels more like a burden to you at the moment, but there are so many wonderful things you can do with your gifts. Come back tomorrow and I'll show you something remarkable; something only we Guardians of Dreamers can do."

I left the store and meandered my way back up Hidden Lane. I half wished he hadn't told me about the Mother of All Nightmares. And I didn't know what gifts could possibly make up for being dreamless. In fact, being a Guardian of Dreamers made me feel as though I was even weirder than Roxy Patterson told everyone I was.

CHAPTER 7

Every single teacher yelled at me today. It had been impossible to concentrate on a single word they'd said – and it wasn't because of Roxy Patterson, for once, because she was off sick.

I couldn't stop thinking about the Book of Dreams and the Book of Nightmares. About Myrdina, desperate to break into our world. The black mask grinning. Was I really a Guardian of Dreamers? It sounded like something out of a Marvel comic. That morning, I'd stared at myself in the bathroom mirror for so long, Dad had knocked on the door to ask if I was OK. I thought I might somehow appear different, but I still had eyes the colour of Galaxy Minstrels, hair as black as a Liquorice Catherine Wheel, a squint fringe and a worried expression on my face. Being a Guardian of Dreamers didn't change the fact that I had a bully on my back and a best friend who didn't want anything to do with me. I longed to sit on our bench in the park and tell Jeannie everything, but she was Roxy's pal now. And anyway, it all sounded so far-fetched and scary, I doubt she'd believe me.

Even though Roxy wasn't there to chase me after school, today was the fastest I'd run to the Dream Store – not even the raindrops could catch me.

As I charged through the door, Sausage landed on a plinth. *"Hello, sailor,"* she said.

Grinning at the bird, I took off my coat. I tried to push down the pang of longing when I saw the bottles. I might not be able to dream, but, according to Mr Curley, there were other things I could do that were special.

Mr Curley stuck his head through the curtains. "Ollo, you've been with us for a while now and I'm impressed with all your hard work. I need to make a new batch of Pirate Arrrrdventure DreamDrops and could do with some assistance. Think you're up to it?"

"I'm the very person, Mr Curley!" Being shown how to make a dream was the next best thing to actually having one.

"Aye-aye, Captain! Avast, ye scurvy dog!" Sausage corkscrewed around the store, chuckling and shedding black feathers everywhere.

"Excellent!" Mr Curley jogged down the stairs to the basement and opened a door leading out into a courtyard. The long grass lining the path waved in the breeze. Swallows screamed above us, performing more daring acrobatics than the Red Arrows. There was a lovely calm feeling as if we were deep in the heart of the countryside. Even the rain pattering on leaves was soothing.

In front of us were two outbuildings: one with a red door and one with a silver door.

Mr Curley strode over to the red door.

"Mr Curley and Ms Ollo," he said. There was a pause and then the door opened. "Welcome to

Dream HQ, where I make all the essences for the DreamDrops."

I stared in awe. There was a long wooden workbench. Against the walls were multicoloured drawers of all shapes and sizes that teetered up to the ceiling, which was made from glass. I gazed up at the clouds as they whipped past, the same colour as a pencil nib.

"What do you know about magic, Ollo?" asked Mr Curley, taking his jacket off and placing it over a chair.

"I once made a coin vanish in a party trick, but that was only because I sneezed by accident."

He smiled. "What exists within these four walls are all the ingredients you need to weave the magic of dreams, something only Guardians can do."

An indigo drawer pushed itself open next to me. Inside it were some strawberry laces.

"Are those for *me*, Mr Curley?" I asked, astonished.

"Dream HQ is welcoming you, Ollo. You'll soon see the place always knows what you need. You could say it works in mysterious ways."

I took the strawberry laces and put them in my

rucksack.

Mr Curley opened a sturdy yellow drawer that was full of glass bottles, laid out on their sides.

I joined him, peering at the labels and marvelling at their names: *Enchanted Wood Sprinkles, Giggle Dust, Mountain Seed, Cloud Generator, Wing Paste* and *Talking Plant Powder.*

"Where did they come from?" I said, my voice filled with wonder.

"I've collected some of them on my travels. The rest are so precious they have been passed down from previous Guardians of Dreamers."

I picked up a small bottle with *Essence of Oceans* written on it.

"Don't drop that, whatever you do! There's enough water in there to flood the whole country! Some of the ingredients are active and must be handled with the utmost care." Mr Curley took the bottle from me and placed it safely back in the drawer.

I wrinkled my nose up. "Mr Curley? Is there *real* magic in the bottles?"

"Let's see, shall we?" He ran his finger along

them and selected one labelled *Snowfall*. He took out the tiniest pinch of white crystals and threw it into the air.

Plump snowflakes drifted down from the ceiling.

I laughed as I twirled around under them, sticking my tongue out so they melted on it. This was no trick of the light; it was real! Within seconds, Dream HQ turned into a winter wonderland with soft peaks of sparkling snow and gleaming icicles that hung from the drawers. Sausage busied herself making snow angels on the worktop and Mr Curley playfully threw a snowball at her. The bird squawked, zoomed up to an overhang of snow, flicked her wing and knocked it on to Mr Curley's head. A deep purple drawer opened with a Brazil nut and two mugs of cocoa. Mr Curley passed me one and I cupped it in my hands for warmth, breathing in the delicious smell. Sausage swooped down for her nut.

The snow began to melt away, until there was none. "Mr Curley, that was AMAZING. I'm sorry I didn't believe you!" I said.

"That's quite all right. In today's world so

many have ceased to believe in the existence of magic that it can prevent it from happening." He brushed the last of the snow from his hair, still rosy-cheeked from the cold. "When you work with dreams, you soon understand there are no limits to the imagination and anything is possible. Now, what can you tell me about Pirate Arrrrdventure DreamDrops?"

I'd heard so many people talking about it at school, I knew the plot by heart. "It's a race-against-time adventure to solve clues and be the first to find the buried treasure before any other pirates do."

He beamed at me. "To make the essence, you need to paint a picture of what is in the dream with words and bring it alive with your senses."

I shifted my weight from one foot to the other. "I'm not sure I'm a real Guardian of Dreamers because I don't know what you mean."

"If you were there, in the dream, what would you see?"

"Um . . . seagulls?"

"That's correct, Ollo. There are bound to be all sorts of birds, common as well as exotic, in the adventure, and all you have to do is tell Dream HQ."

"That's it? Just say what I think you'd find in the dream?"

"Why don't you give it a whirl?" Mr Curley sat in an armchair, waiting for me to begin.

"OK," I said cautiously. I couldn't see how this would work. Still, I would give it a try.

I closed my eyes and imagined I was in the dream, which was easy because I did it every night. "There is a sparkling clear blue ocean that smells of salt. I can feel hot sunshine on my skin and soft white sand beneath my feet." I heard a scraping noise and looked to see what it was. Drawers were opening all around the room and Mr Curley was collecting bottles from them. I closed my eyes and continued. "There are vast ships with rigging, crow's nests and black cannons, a wobbly gangplank, wooden rowing boats to get from the ship to shore, a wrinkled treasure map, a motley crew of pirates with patches over their eyes, striped tops, wooden legs and gleaming silver cutlass swords. There are uncharted waters filled with whales and sea monsters, and mysterious caves to explore – and lush tropical islands with palm trees, multicoloured parrots, chattering monkeys, circling sharks and a mountain of buried gold and precious jewels. Oh, and there would be rum by the bucketload, because pirates don't drink anything else."

"Ahoy, matey! Shiver me timbers!" cried out Sausage.

"Ollo! You've taken to this like a duck to water. You're a natural – except for the rum, which doesn't mix well with children in charge of a large seafaring vessel on choppy waters. I usually give them lemonade."

I grinned sheepishly and placed the Barrels of Rum Cordial back in a green drawer that squeaked as it closed.

"There are a few more things I suggest we add, Ollo. We need Spanish Galleon Ship Oil, so children can experience what it really was like to explore the ocean on an original wooden vessel. I'm going to pop in Constellation Dust, so they can learn to navigate using the stars, and a generous sprinkle of Spirit of Adventure – as this allows all children to shed their worries, self-doubt and shyness to become wild and free, which is how they should be. And we mustn't forget the wind for the sails, otherwise the ship won't be going anywhere," said Mr Curley.

I grabbed a silver flask labelled Four Winds from a deep wooden drawer, and popped its lid off. A long grey swirl shot out and filled the room with a howling gale. Before Sausage could take cover, she was blown off the bench into a drawer which shut.

Mr Curley yelled something, but I couldn't hear him over the roar of the wind.

I held on to the worktop for dear life and reached out with my other hand to cover the jug, so we wouldn't lose what we'd already mixed.

Mr Curley let go of the bench and tumbled across the floor to the other side of the room, where he was pinned against some drawers. With great effort, he managed to stand and, gripping on to the drawer handles, pulled himself back to the bench and the Four Winds flask. As he neared it, he launched himself over it, sealing it off.

The wind dropped and everything that had been up in the air fell to the floor with a crash. "Ollo, find the lid for Four Winds!" he rasped.

I searched everywhere, eventually spotting it on the top of a crooked stack of orange drawers.

I handed it to Mr Curley, who swiftly stoppered the bottle. He leaned on the bench, exhausted, his hair standing on end.

A drawer with leaves stencilled on it opened next to him and Mr Curley pulled out a comb. "Most thoughtful of you, Dream HQ," he said, smiling.

The blue drawer opposite me began to ring like a doorbell, so I rushed around to investigate.

Sausage flew out, landed on the worktop and shook herself. *"Holy . . ."*

"Language, Sausage!" interrupted Mr Curley.

"I'm really sorry, Mr Curley," I said. "I had no idea that was going to happen."

"Some of the live ingredients must be manipulated before they're removed from their containers, so I put them into my blast chiller." He took me over to what looked like a microwave, popped the Four Winds flask inside it and jabbed at some buttons.

"Substances like wind, fire, clouds, lightning and oceans must be frozen before being taken out of their containers so they won't wreak too much havoc." There was a *ping* and Mr Curley brought it back out. The flask was now full of ice crystals, which he chipped into the Pirate Arrrrdventure mixture.

I scuffed the floor with my toe.

"No harm done, Ollo. My first ever mishap was a mudslide, and that took weeks to clean up afterwards. Mistakes are wonderful things because they teach us what not to do. There's one more ingredient to put in: lastly, and most importantly, we need to add Nightmare Repellent to keep the dreamers protected from Myrdina."

A slim metal drawer opened and I fetched a black bottle of liquid. Mr Curley added one drop of it to the jug, making the contents fizz so violently, I thought they'd spill over the top. He waited until it settled before he stirred it.

"And there we have it: Pirate Arrrrdventure DreamDrop essence."

"*Ta-dah!*" squawked Sausage.

I gazed at it, enchanted by the way it rose and fell inside the jug, just like the sea. As I leaned in for a closer look, I could have sworn I heard seagulls crying, voices singing a shanty song and the crash of waves against the shore. Curious, I wondered what it tasted of. I dipped my finger into the blue liquid and raised it to my lips.

"Ollo!" yelled Mr Curley. "Please remember to exercise great caution at all times."

I dropped my hand down by my side, startled.

"Knickers," said Sausage.

"If you have a dream, there's a possibility the Mother of All Nightmares could sense you were a Guardian of Dreamers and try to use you to escape from her world into this one."

"But how would she know who I was?"

"She doesn't know who you are, but to her you smell different from other children, and it's feasible she might guess what you are."

I stood, looking at my feet.

"Ollo, as I've already mentioned, making mistakes is the best way for us to learn." Mr Curley patted my arm. "I think that's quite enough magic for now."

I glanced around the workshop, which was a mess.

"Mr Curley, would you like me to tidy up?"

"Dream HQ can clean itself."

"*Really?* I *wish* my bedroom could do that."

"Come on, we'll take the essence to the Dream Factory so I don't run out of drops for the customers."

I held on to the jug of Pirate Arrrrdventure and followed Mr Curley at a snail's pace, careful not to spill it.

Outside, Mr Curley ordered Sausage to stay put in the courtyard.

"She isn't allowed in the factory because of the machinery," he explained. "This makes her most ill-tempered."

The mynah bird glided over to a tree blowing raspberries.

Mr Curley announced our names to the silver door and we entered a windowless building the size of a gym hall. Strip lights hung from the ceiling and there was a deafening clack and whir of machinery. A steel vat hissed as steam escaped from the top of it. From a spout poured a long thin stream of white-hot liquid that was chopped into pieces that were then shaped into tiny treasure chests. The drops were stamped with the Dream Store's cloud-shaped logo and passed under a fan to cool and harden.

I moved closer, fascinated.

"Watch out, Ollo," Mr Curley warned. "We have an alarm system. There are laser beams around the machinery, invisible to the eye. They're sensitive, so if anything larger than a fly is near the drops, I'll know about it. I simply can't have any impurities in the children's dreams."

Hundreds of Pirate Arrrrdventure drops whizzed past. Hundreds of exhilarating, adventure-filled dreams.

Mr Curley took the jug from me and climbed the ladder on the side of the vat to pour the essence in. "This should be enough for at least another four hundred bottles," he yelled before he came back down, hopping off the last rung. He inhaled some steam and sneezed. Bringing out his handkerchief to blow his nose, he scattered Brazil nuts everywhere.

"All in all, I think we've done a good afternoon's work, Ollo. Let's go, shall we?" He strode off along the side of the conveyor belt.

I took one last look at the drops, each one a reminder of a dream I would never have.

I dragged my feet along the path back to the basement.

"What's the matter, Ollo?" asked Mr Curley.

"You've never had a dream either, have you?"

"No – we have that in common. I know it can sometimes be challenging being around the drops at first. But Ollo, you must never take one, otherwise the consequences would be dire. Promise me that if you're ever tempted by them, you'll come and tell me immediately."

I thought of Seraphina, warning me I was *never to give in to temptation*, and an iciness trickled through my veins.

"I promise, Mr Curley," I said. We entered the basement and I picked up a paperweight with a butterfly in it. "Did other children treat you differently because you couldn't dream?"

"Very much so," he said. "Being different is sometimes as much of a curse as it is a blessing. Ollo, we might not be able to dream at night – but we can do something even better. We can dream during the day and use our imaginations to keep children happy and safe from Myrdina."

I thought about the Book of Nightmares and that grinning mask and my stomach lurched. Myrdina scared me stiff.

"Can we mix more dreams tomorrow, Mr Curley? It's the best thing I've ever done in my whole life."

Sausage honked like an old car horn.

"Ollo, I want you to do something very important. I showed you Dream HQ and the Dream Factory so you'd understand how everything works here. What I want you to do now is to come up with some amazing dreams of your own."

"Me?" The paperweight slipped from my grasp, but I managed to catch it in time. I placed it back on the shelf. "Why me?"

"You're young, so you know exactly what children will love. I think it's high time we had a new perspective around here."

Sausage hopped up and down, making the noises of rockets and bangers going off.

I remembered Roxy Patterson hurling my school bag over a fence on to the railway tracks and dropping my art project into the river. If I had as good an imagination as Mr Curley thought, I'd have figured out how to get her off my back ages ago.

I chewed my lip.

"Ollo, doubting oneself is the biggest killer of imagination." Mr Curley paced up and down the rug. "And we need more dreams for the children to buy. The Book of Dreams is slowing down again. When I checked the Book of Nightmares I found it has been more active; it hardly stopped all night. If Myrdina is plotting something, I will need your help. All I'm asking is that you come back tomorrow with some ideas for dreams you've always wanted to have and we'll take it from there." Mr Curley opened a cupboard and brought out a Dream Store notebook and pen. Sausage settled on Mr Curley's shoulder and nibbled his ear.

My heart played pinball around my ribs.

The thought of creating a dream good enough to keep children safe was daunting.

"I'll give it a go, Mr Curley, but I can't promise anything." I took the pad and pen from him and put them in my rucksack.

After dinner I went to my room, cleared some mugs and a plate off my desk and sat with my DreamDrops pen. It released a bubblegum-smelling perfume when I clicked it. Nibbling on a strawberry lace, I decided that compiling a list of dreams would be the best way to start. I wrote the numbers one to five on the paper and busied myself filling them in with doodles of a boy knight on his horse. I sighed and checked my phone, just in case Jeannie had called or sent a message – but there was nothing.

My eyes settled on the wall by the window. I'd been allowed to draw on it because Mum had said the room needed to be redecorated anyway – but we'd never got around to it. Jeannie and I had sketched pictures of ourselves with our shades and matching red trainers on, looking way cooler than we actually were. She'd written *Best friends 4 ever* underneath it.

I missed her so much it hurt like broken bones.

It was no use.

None of this was helping me come up with something good.

I couldn't think of any dreams.

My heart sank as I imagined arriving at the Dream Store empty-handed. Mr Curley would realize I was *hopeless*, Sausage would regret persuading him to interview me for the job and they'd tell me to go away and never come back again.

I swept the pad and pen off my desk into the wastepaper basket.

I didn't want to be a Guardian of Dreamers. I wanted to have a dream with a knight and a dragon. I wanted to learn how to be brave and strong and protect myself against Roxy.

I glanced out the window. The night sky was peppered with so many stars it reminded me of the snow flurry in Dream HQ. Making the DreamDrops was the best thing I'd ever done. I couldn't let Mr Curley down – not after he'd been so kind to me. And if I came up with something good, it could help keep children safe from Myrdina. Plus the extra money would come in handy because Mum and Dad had been arguing over the bills lately.

I fished around in the wastepaper basket for my pen and notebook, then brought them back out. I tucked the chair in closer to the desk, sat straight and smoothed the page down. Even if it took me all night, I would fill it with ideas. And after school tomorrow, I was going to give Mr Curley the best dreams he'd ever seen.

CHAPTER 8

"Show yourself, freak, or I'm coming in to get you."

All I could glimpse of Roxy Patterson were her green DMs through the gap under the toilet door.

Time had passed slowly that day, as if the clocks were going backwards. I couldn't stop thinking about showing Mr Curley my dreams. When the end of the day had finally arrived, I'd hidden in the loos after the school bell, so I could dodge Roxy Patterson at the gates. Unfortunately she'd seen me go in, and now I was stuck in a cubicle, surrounded by Roxy and her gang, all of them whispering.

I looked frantically around. There was a small window but it was painted shut. Mr Curley would be wondering where I was soon.

Roxy banged on the door with a fist.

I shuffled away into the furthest corner.

"You're a total waste of space. You've no brain, you hang out in toilets, and you've no friends. You're so pathetic you can't even dream," she said.

Roxy Patterson began throwing herself at the door, wheezing.

Toilet roll was hardly going to protect me from a crazy person.

The smell of the loos and Roxy's sickly perfume made my empty stomach slide and tip as though I was at sea.

I heard the sound of taps being turned on and fought the urge to climb on the toilet seat to see what they were up to. After some giggling, five pairs of feet gathered outside the cubicle.

Without warning, wet paper towels were launched over the top of the door, followed by a bin full of water, emptied over my head.

I shrieked at the shock of its iciness and stood

with my arms out from my sides, spitting water from my mouth. My hair clung to my face, my shirt stuck to my skin and my skirt dripped faster than a leaky tap. The water pooled on the floor.

The girls roared with laughter. "I'm going to get you, sooner than you think," said Roxy Patterson.

I watched their feet walking away. The door to the toilets squealed open and then shut, and I could hear their voices outside in the corridor.

There was silence.

I picked up my sodden rucksack. Just then, someone came into the bathroom. *"Hello?"*

I'd know that voice anywhere. Sometimes our mums couldn't even tell us apart on the phone.

I grabbed some toilet paper and patted it over my hair and face.

"Ollo? Is that you? Are you OK?" said Jeannie. "It's only me."

I unlocked the door and stepped out.

Jeannie covered her mouth with her hand at the sight of me and then flicked her eyes over to the door.

And I spied Roxy Patterson.

Jeannie had tricked me.

I glared at them, my blood hissing in my ears.

Jeannie stared back at me as though I was a stranger. As if we'd never made promises to be friends for ever. Become so close, we could finish off each other's sentences. We'd even bought the same pairs of red trainers, loving how we matched as we chased each other through the park.

Jeannie's shoes were green now.

The spilled water changed the toilet floor into a glasslike surface.

"Told you I'd get you sooner than you thought." Roxy lunged to grab me and I ducked to the side. Her foot skidded in the water and she shot forward at speed, smacking her face straight into the sink. Roxy fell backwards, crashing to the ground; a thin line of red trickled down her chin.

Jeannie gasped and knelt at her side. "Look what you've done, Ollo!"

"I didn't touch her," I said. "You saw what happened. That wasn't my fault."

Roxy made a gurgling noise, coughed and spat out a tooth.

I started to shake.

"Don't move, Roxy. I'll get help." Jeannie leapt up, grabbed me by the arm and dragged me out of the toilets.

"You need to leave," she said, her eyes scanning the corridor for a teacher. "Roxy will kill you for this."

I sprinted away from Jeannie and launched myself out through the doors, gulping in the fresh air.

I sped through the gates and hurtled down the steps at the end of the street, sending starlings spiralling skywards.

I'd done it now.

An angry Roxy was a dangerous enemy to have. She wouldn't give up until she had taught me a lesson. And Jeannie knew all my hiding places at school and in the park.

Fear made my skin prickle. I didn't want to end up in hospital – or worse – because of Roxy.

A grey car flashed past me.

I thought of the boy knight's armour gleaming as he stood strong and fearless in front of the dragon.

The way he'd twirled his swords and conquered the creature without even breaking into a sweat. If the knight could show me how to defend myself against the dragon, I would have a chance of standing up to Roxy Patterson. With Jeannie no longer my friend, and nobody else here to help, having a dream was my only hope of getting out of this alive.

I turned into Hidden Lane and halted when I saw the Dream Store. Mr Curley's words came back to me about never having a dream otherwise I could set Myrdina free. There was no way I could do that and put so many children in Parradicehill at risk. He'd said she'd know what I was by my smell. A thought sprang to mind: if I masked my scent, the Mother of All Nightmares would never know I was a Guardian of Dreamers! And the knight could teach me all his moves without me worrying about anyone being harmed – or Mr Curley finding out about what I had done.

Someone yelled and I jumped, checking the lane for Roxy, but she was nowhere in sight.

I was fed up of living in fear. I was going to steal some A Knight's Adventure DreamDrops and learn how to defend myself in my very first ever dream – tonight.

Even though I'd stopped running, my heart still beat fast. I trembled as I entered the store, certain Mr Curley would guess what I was up to the minute he saw me.

The shop was empty: Mr Curley and Sausage were nowhere to be seen.

I darted over to the A Knight's Adventure bottles, my trainers lighting the tiles and making squeaks on the floor. I snatched up a bottle.

"Ollo! What a pity! We've just finished making a batch of A Knight's Adventure essence." Mr Curley put down a box of DreamDrops he was carrying.

Sausage hopped over the floor, singing. *"I'm late, I'm late, for a very important date."*

I slipped the bottle back on to the shelf. "I'm sorry, Mr Curley, the teacher kept me behind after class." I could have kicked myself. I had missed out on the opportunity to make the very dream I was after.

Mr Curley stared at me and I squirmed. I must

have looked pretty bedraggled. "I hope you weren't in any trouble?"

"Not me, Mr Curley. I'm always good as gold."

Sausage blew a raspberry and flew on to a plinth to clean her wings.

Mr Curley was still eyeballing me. "Has it been raining?" he asked.

I must have looked as though I'd been for a swim fully clothed in the river.

"It was bucketing down earlier, Mr Curley," I said, grimly. My breath caught in the back of my throat.

"Is everything quite all right?" Mr Curley blinked several times in a row.

"I'm just worried about whether the dreams I've come up with are any good." I patted my rucksack.

His face relaxed. "There is no such thing as a bad idea, Ollo. Let's take a look at what you've done and put you out of your misery." He locked the door and we went to the basement.

"Would you like some tea and lemon drizzle cake?" Mr Curley asked.

"No thanks, Mr Curley." The thought of Roxy Patterson coming for me had shrivelled my stomach to the size of an ant.

Mr Curley sat on the sofa and drummed his fingers on the seat while he waited for me to fish out my notebook. Sausage settled behind him so she could read over his shoulder.

I took a deep breath and passed the book to Mr Curley, who began to flick through the pages.

After what seemed like ages, he shut it.

Sausage shook her head and wiped her beak on the sofa.

I scratched my ankle. "What do you think, Mr Curley?"

He pursed his lips. "None of them made any sense, Ollo."

"*Poubelle,*" croaked Sausage.

My face fell. I'd put every single piece of imagination I had into those dreams.

Mr Curley opened the notebook and held it up for me to see.

The page was as wrinkled as skin in a bath and covered in a series of blue and purple ink smudges, making the words impossible to read. The entire notebook had been ruined by the water.

"Just as well it's all up here, Mr Curley," I said, tapping my head. I leapt up and hurried over to a pinboard on the wall next to the sofas.

Sausage landed on the shelf above me and did a dance.

There was a pen and a stack of paper on the side. I began writing down all my ideas again. Ten minutes later, I put the pen down and pinned the sheets of paper to the board.

Mr Curley approached and stood with his hands clasped behind his back as he read through everything. I couldn't bear to watch him, so I went over to the window and looked out into the courtyard.

If Mr Curley had made a batch of A Knight's Adventure essence, that meant the drops might be in the factory. All I had to do was slip in and pinch one off the conveyor belt. Surely Mr Curley wouldn't notice.

"Ollo?"

I whirled around, scared Mr Curley had read my thoughts.

"These are exceptional." His face was alight. "A Novel Adventure, where you can meet your favourite characters from a book and explore their world with them, is inspired. It's got bestseller written all over it. It would take complex magic, but Dream HQ is full of surprises and more than capable of it."

"Thanks, Mr Curley," I said. I could feel my ears going pink. "I worked harder on these than I've ever done on my homework."

"And Planet You is marvellous. Children can travel inside their own bodies! It's the perfect mix of yucky, sensational and educational in equal measure, which is why it'll go down a storm." He held out another piece of paper. "'Best Friends 4 Ever: friends change; they come and go, but one friend will always be with you through thick and thin.' I've only picked out a few but there's something in each and every one of these ideas."

I glowed. And for just the briefest second, I forgot all about Roxy Patterson.

A banging noise interrupted us.

"Oh, I'm expecting a delivery!" said Mr Curley.

"Wait here, we have much to discuss." He left, his footsteps echoing on the stairs.

"I won't move a muscle, Mr Curley. I'll be on the sofa the whole time," I called after him.

Roxy Patterson would be raging by now. If I wanted the knight to teach me how to defend myself against her, this was the perfect time to get my hands on the drops.

The sound of Mr Curley greeting someone at the door floated down into the basement.

I let myself out into the courtyard and raced across the path, alarming pigeons that filled the air with a sharp clap of wings. I glanced behind me to see if anyone had noticed, but nobody was at the window.

Sausage followed me into the courtyard and sat in a tree, watching.

I reached the silver door of the Dream Factory and whispered my name, my voice shaky.

Nothing happened.

I repeated my name, this time loud and clear.

I felt my heart beat in my throat.

The door slid open and I slipped inside, feeling

like a burglar. I gulped. I *was* a burglar. Steam belched from the metal vat, the dusty floor vibrated as the machinery clacked and thousands of white drops in the shapes of shields whizzed past me. They had to be A Knight's Adventure DreamDrops!

I followed them along the conveyor belt down to where the bottles were filled with the drops. There were no security tags on them.

Why not make this worth my while and go for a whole bottle?

I reached my out my hand and then snatched it back, cursing. Mr Curley had told me there were laser beams around the machinery. I'd very nearly set off an alarm.

I was going to have to work out where the beams were before I could pinch a bottle, otherwise Mr Curley would know exactly what I was up to and he'd never trust me again, because I'd lost count of the number of times he'd warned me not to take the drops.

Thing was, how did you find invisible beams?

On my way back to the door to check where Mr Curley was, my foot caught on a tangle of cables and I fell face down on the floor. I lifted my head, annoyed at myself for being so clumsy. That's when I noticed the dust I'd stirred up had highlighted a whole bunch of thin red lines that were crisscrossed around the machinery.

I could see the lasers!

I ran to the door and spotted a movement at the window. Mr Curley was signing for the delivery.

Sausage swooped down from the tree and hopped sideways over to me. As I gave her a nervous smile, she pecked at my foot, which made me yelp, and then in a flurry of wingbeats she slipped past me into the Dream Factory.

It wasn't safe for her! And if she got too close to the machines, she'd set off every alarm in the place!

I scooted inside to find the bird perched on a stack of boxes near the door. Opposite her, I spotted the Brazil nuts Mr Curley had dropped and bent to scoop them up.

"If you've never had a dream before, the drops become unstable and can conjure up a nightmare so bad, your life, as well as many others, would be in danger," said Mr Curley.

I froze.

I'd been caught red-handed.

I straightened up and turned around slowly – only to find Mr Curley wasn't there; it was Sausage.

The bird had mimicked his voice to stop me!

I waggled the nuts in the air to lure her over. My heart missed some beats as she flew towards the conveyor belt and then changed direction at the very last moment to land on the floor next to me. I broke the nuts into pieces and laid a trail of them leading out of the Dream Factory. Sausage pecked at them until she was once again in the courtyard. Breathing a sigh of relief, I shut the door. The mynah bird opened her beak and the deafening noise of a police siren ripped through the air.

I'd have seconds before Mr Curley appeared. I sprinted down the side of the conveyor belt, grabbed some dust from the floor and threw it up into the air. In that instant, I could see three beams crisscrossing the machinery. My hand snaked under two of them and stopped short of the third. I waggled my fingers and caught hold of a bottle of the DreamDrops, stuck it into my pocket and bolted towards the door.

Seraphina's words had come to me then. *Never give in to temptation or there will be terrible consequences.* Beads of sweat collected on my forehead.

The door to the Dream Factory closed behind me and I clocked Mr Curley at the top of the stairs. I rushed past the trees as Sausage dive-bombed me, still wailing like a siren. Racing into the basement, I skidded past the table, chucked the DreamDrops into my rucksack and threw myself on to the sofa, crossing my legs as if I'd been there the whole time. I snatched up a piece of lemon drizzle cake and put it on my plate.

"Why on earth is Sausage sounding an alarm?" asked Mr Curley, hurrying into the room.

I faced him, trying my best to hide that I was out of breath. "I'm sorry, Mr Curley. It was so tempting, I couldn't resist pinching some." I held out the plate with the cake on it.

Mr Curley laughed.

Sausage circled above our heads, crying out, *"Thief! Thief!"*

"I'm afraid lemon drizzle is her very favourite. Mine too, as it happens." He patted his stomach, which was more hillock than six-pack.

I counted my lucky stars Mr Curley hadn't noticed the dirt on my legs and that the tips of my trainers were coated in dust.

"Mr Curley, would it be OK if I left a bit earlier tonight?"

"Of course, Ollo. I'm impressed at how hard you have worked. Your ideas are wonderful. I'll have a think and decide which we can try out first."

"Really?" I squeaked.

Mr Curley smiled, the lines around his mouth deepening. "The store is always at its busiest on a Saturday, but Sausage can hold the fort for an hour."

Sausage blew a series of long, deep raspberries. *"Thief,"* she muttered angrily.

"I've no idea what's made her so cranky," said Mr Curley, shaking his head.

I walked to the door, clutching my bag like an eagle grips a salmon so the DreamDrops didn't rattle against the glass.

Sausage glared at me as I waved goodbye and fled out into the night, like the thief that I was.

CHAPTER 9

I made it home without running into Roxy Patterson. The last time I'd seen her had been on the wet bathroom floor, with blood on her chin. I was as good as dead if she found me.

The lift doors banged open on the seventeenth floor and I hurried down the corridor towards my flat. As I neared it, a hand gripped my arm, and I whirled around, crying out in fright.

"Am I really that scary without any make-up on?"

"I'm sorry, Seraphina," I said. "You startled me."

Her hair was wrapped in a blue towel with dolphins on it.

"I've spent the afternoon telling fortunes at a hen party. All I wanted was a nice relaxing evening. There I was in the bath, chin-deep in bubbles, surrounded by candles, and all I could hear was spirit voices, whining. I decided to ignore them, fetched a tub of Ben and Jerry's and curled up on the sofa to watch my favourite programme: *Ice Road Truckers*. Could I get any peace and quiet? What do you think?"

I shifted guiltily. "What has this got to do with me?"

"It's got everything to do with you. They're telling you not to give in to temptation, otherwise there will be dire consequences. Does this make sense *now*?"

I clutched my bag, with the drops inside.

"I promise if temptation does come my way, I won't give in to it," I lied.

Seraphina nodded, satisfied with my answer, and glanced up to the heavens. "You hear that? She's going to behave, so can I please watch the telly without any more interruptions?" The medium narrowed her eyes at me. "Whatever you're up to, don't do it, Ollo – but do stop by the café for some cake soon. It'll be on the house."

I managed a thin smile. "I will."

Seraphina walked towards the lifts.

I scooted around the corner and let myself into the flat. I opened the hallway cupboard, kicked my trainers off into it and slung my coat in after them.

"Ollo? There are hot dogs in the oven for your tea," shouted Mum from the kitchen.

"I'm not hungry!" I said as I went straight to my room, breathing a sigh of relief as I slammed the door.

The picture of Jeannie and me fell off my mirror and fluttered to the ground. I didn't bother picking it up.

I changed into my pyjamas, dumping my damp school clothes in a pile on the floor. Climbing into bed, I opened my rucksack and took the DreamDrops out. The drops tinkled softly as my fingers traced around the knight's head and over the flying dragons and swords on the glass.

Electric shivers ran up and down my body.

A knock at the door made my heart stick to the top of my ribcage and I shoved the bottle under my pillow.

"Mum wants to know if you're OK because you don't want anything to eat and normally you're like a human dustbin," said Kyle.

"Go away!" I said.

I waited until I heard the lounge door close before I brought the DreamDrops back out.

My heart thundered faster than a horse on a racing track.

I had imagined this moment for so long, I couldn't believe it was finally happening.

And yet, in my head were the warnings.

Mr Curley, telling me that everything I dreamed of would become real. And that the Mother of All Nightmares would use me to escape the dream world.

Seraphina, speaking for the spirits, telling me not to give in to temptation.

Maybe taking the drops wasn't such a good idea after all.

My phone rang and I kicked my covers back to

grab my rucksack. I fished around inside it, through wet bits of paper, crumbs and fluff sticking to my hands. I found the phone sandwiched between the pages of a textbook and pulled it out to see Jeannie's number on the screen.

I glanced at the photo of us laughing and my anger melted away. Maybe she wanted to apologize for what happened earlier. See if I was OK. It'd be great to hear her voice.

I pressed the button and held the phone to my ear.

The airwaves hissed and crackled.

"Hi, Ollo," said Jeannie. "There's someone here who wants to talk to you."

There was a pause and then I caught the faintest sound of a wheeze.

"You're dead meat, Ollo. I'm coming for you tomorrow," said Roxy.

Laughter spilled out from the phone and I let go of it. Panic rose in my chest. Roxy would hunt me down until she had me cornered, that I was sure of. She even knew where I lived. I took a breath and steadied my thoughts.

Even if Myrdina was terrifying, DreamDrops had Nightmare Repellent, which I was certain would keep me safe. And I felt sure if my scent was covered up, the Mother of All Nightmares would never even know I was there. I could slip in and back out again without her escaping or putting any children in harm's way. Mr Curley would never suspect what I had been up to. The last thing I wanted was to lose my job.

I walked over to the shelves and selected a perfume, which I sprayed myself with from head to toe. It was so overpowering, my eyes stung and I had a coughing fit. I climbed back into bed and twisted the DreamDrops bottle top around until the seal broke with a crack and set the time on it. The knight's visor popped up and a shield-shaped drop slid out on to the palm of my trembling hand.

I put it in my mouth, marvelling at how it tasted. Like strawberry laces, only a million times fruitier. Swallowing the last of it, I put the bottle on my bedside table, switched off my light and lay down, wiggling my toes as I awaited the lightness of sleep so I could have my very first dream.

*

The grass was as green as Milk Choc Block Quality Street wrappers, and it tickled. Every cloud in the sky glowed white as mashed potato with perfect scalloped tops and flat bottoms exactly the same as the Dream Store's logo.

This was nothing like the park in Parradicehill.

Everything was more colourful and there was no litter, graffiti or dog poo bags anywhere.

I was really doing it. I was having my very first dream.

I sprang to my feet, whirling around in a circle, whooping.

Behind me was a sapphire-blue lake with a postcard-pretty village nestled on its far shores. In front of me, a path wound its way past flowers and trees towards a forest.

I cartwheeled over to the path where I walked along until I came to a bridge that was perfect for Poohsticks, a game Kyle and I loved when we were little. The river flowed over giant rocks, and as I peered into the pools below I could see the shapes of fish hugging the sides of the bank. There were no rusty shopping trolleys here.

Opposite the bridge was an entranceway into some dark, creaking woods. I hesitated. This was A Knight's Adventure and there could be creatures with big teeth in there. Not to mention, it was the kind of place you'd expect the Mother of All Nightmares to be hiding.

The sooner I found the boy knight, the better.

"Hello? Anyone there?" I shouted, my voice tiny in such a vast open space.

Nobody appeared.

An idea came to me. Dad loved watching Westerns and the cowboys sometimes whistled to call their horses. I put my fingers to my mouth and blew as hard as I could.

Up ahead, a black horse sailed out of the woods. The horse galloped towards me and the knight's armour gleamed like polished taps. As they came to a halt, the boy swung himself down from his horse, dropped his shield and removed his helmet.

"Bertrand Ponce de Leon, at your service," he said with a bow.

The knight was tall and broad with a head of HP Sauce–coloured curls that had been squished flat under the helmet. He had a large freckle slap-bang between his Slush Puppie–blue eyes that was hard to stop staring at and a dimple on his chin. He wore a navy tunic, double-belted at the waist. Emblazoned across his chest was a green dragon, breathing fire, and at each hip hung a silver sword. At a guess, he must have been fourteen because if he'd been any older, he would probably have spots, stink of aftershave and be a smart alec, like Kyle.

I marched up to him and knocked on the armour plating protecting his shoulders. It gave a hollow tin-can sound. I smiled, satisfied he wasn't a projection or trick of the light.

The knight glanced at me out of the corner of his eye.

His horse flicked its tail and chomped on the lush grass.

"Can I pat him?" It was something I'd always longed to do because there weren't many horses hanging around Parradicehill.

Bertrand stepped to one side.

The horse towered over me with a coat as shiny as black patent leather. I stood on my tiptoes and drew my fingers along the arch of his damp neck, rubbing behind his ears. He had eyes as brown as chestnuts and eyelashes so long, Mum would have killed for them. The horse pawed the ground and then snorted, blowing my fringe to the side. He also let off the second loudest fart I'd ever heard in my life.

"What's his name?" I said.

"Lantern. May I enquire what yours is?"

"Ollo."

"How charming."

My shoulders stooped a little. "You don't need to be polite. Everyone at school thinks it's weird."

"I've not heard anything like it before. Does it have a noble meaning?"

"I doubt it."

"Do you have your big boots on, Ollo?"

"I only brought my slippers. Why?"

"Because we're about to embark on the adventure of a lifetime." When the knight smiled, his teeth were so impossibly white they looked like something out of a toothpaste advert.

I fidgeted. "Could I ask for your assistance with something else instead?"

"And what would that be?" He loosened his belt a notch.

I swatted away a fly. "I want you to show me how to fight off the school bully who is going to kill me tomorrow because she blames me for knocking her front tooth out."

"We're supposed to be defending that village over there from a dragon attack that's going to happen in approximately forty minutes' time." Bert cast his gaze across the gleaming lake.

I lowered my head. It hadn't occurred to me the knight might not want to help me.

I'd risked everything to take the DreamDrops, all for nothing.

Before my eyes had time to well up, the knight placed his hand under my chin and tilted it back up.

"This request is highly unusual, Lady Ollo." He waggled his eyebrows. "Luckily for you, I've sworn an oath and cannot refuse a damsel in distress." Bert leaned in closer and then sniffed the air. "Whatever is that smell?"

"Enchantment," I said, happy the perfume was strong enough for him to notice. "My granny gave it to me for my birthday. Do you like it?"

"On the bright side, I'm sure it'll repel dragons," replied Bert. "Now, where was I?"

"You were saying you can't refuse a damsel in distress."

"Ah, yes! If you need help fighting a dastardly enemy, I'm your knight."

I'm not sure I could have fit a bigger grin on my face.

"Come, Lady Ollo!" He tied his helmet to the saddlebag. "We shall go to my camp in Eldermere Forest, where I will teach you the basics of camouflage, ambush, self-defence and how to gut the enemy with one flick of the sword."

I wanted Roxy Patterson to end up scared of me rather than dead, but seeing as how it was my first dream, I thought it would be OK to flag this up with Bertrand later on.

The knight grabbed his shield, leapt on to

Lantern and held out his hand. I took it and in one swift move, he swung me up on to the horse. He'd clearly been eating lots of porridge, which Dad told me made you really strong.

"Bertrand?" I said, nervous I was sitting high up on a huge horse without a seat belt.

"Yes, Lady Ollo?" he replied.

"Can I call you Bert?"

"If it pleases you." Bert clicked his tongue at Lantern and pulled on the reins, so we faced the entrance to the forest.

The slight movement made me cling on to him for dear life.

"There's no need to call me *Lady* because I'm not a real one. I'm just a girl who is in a whole lot of trouble at the moment."

"I shall bear this in mind, Lady Ollo." Bert rose off the saddle, tilted forward, shouted *hup*, and we took off like the wind, with my eyes firmly shut.

CHAPTER 10

In the forest, Bert slowed the horse to a trot, I coughed as I'd forgotten to close my mouth and swallowed a couple of insects along the way. The woods were thick and dark, with the tallest trees I'd ever seen. In Parradicehill most of the trees were plastic, decorated in fairy lights or just stumps. Giant shafts of light speared through the leaves, highlighting the forest floor in golden patches that shrank and grew in the breeze. In amongst the tangles of ferns, shrubs and flowers, rabbits flashed their white tails and deer bounded across our path.

The pigeons were twice the size they were back home and not covered in soot with stumpy feet.

I sniffed the air, which was warm, and scented with pine and toffee apples.

"The trees smell so good here, Bert."

The knight half turned his head. "Ollo, we must stop so Lantern can drink. Carrying two of us is thirsty work."

That was fine by me. All the galloping had made my bum ache.

I wished I'd worn jeans instead of pyjamas.

Bert dismounted from the horse and helped me down to the ground. My legs trembled because I'd been gripping on to Lantern with my knees.

"Is that your house motto?" he asked, glancing at my red pyjama top, which had *Girls just wanna have fun* emblazoned across it.

"It is," I answered with a shrug. "Do you have one?"

"*Potius ingenio quam vi.* It's Latin for *Rather by skill than force.*"

It was then I knew Bert was the knight for me and taking the drops had been, without a doubt, the right thing to do. I'd never be strong enough to fight off Roxy Patterson because she was three times my size, but if I could outsmart her, I was in with a chance.

"Are you thirsty?" Bert undid his saddlebag and brought out a bottle made from leather.

I took a sip and immediately spat it out, spraying liquid everywhere.

"What is *that*?" I wiped my tongue with my sleeve.

"Mead – it's only honeyed wine."

"*Seriously?* You need to get your hands on some Fanta or Sprite." I glared at Bert.

The knight led Lantern to the stream, where the horse stooped to take a drink.

A pea-green bird with a call like a firework landed on the tree above me, and jumped from branch to branch. Wondering what it could be, I craned my neck up, trying to get a better view of it. Feeling dizzy, I stepped back, lost my footing and tumbled down a steep embankment littered with branches, holly leaves, brambles and pine cones. I stood, hoping I hadn't been seen. I found myself in a clearing with a dark green cottage made out of ivy at the end of it.

I was about to scramble back up the embankment when I heard a girl's muffled voice.

"Somebody, please, help me?"

I froze.

"I know you're there," said a girl's voice. "Heard you crashing down the embankment like an elephant. If you'd gone a bit further along to the right, you'd have seen there are steps."

The voice sounded as though it was coming from inside the ivy cottage.

"Hello?" I said, feeling stupid talking to a cottage.

"I can tell by your voice that you are a very kind and thoughtful person."

I brushed some earth from my sleeves. "I think I am."

I studied the building. The ivy was knotted tight around the entire cottage and appeared to be squeezing the life out of it, like a python.

A nagging feeling bubbled up in my stomach that something wasn't right. I pushed the niggle away because this wasn't Parradicehill: this was A

Knight's Adventure, where everything was new and strange and brilliant.

"I'm Dina. What's your name?" asked the girl.

"Ollo," I said, waiting for her to snigger, but she didn't.

"I'm in a spot of bother, Ollo. I spilled a potion by accident on the ivy that was meant for the vegetable patch to make things grow fast. It's gone haywire and now I'm trapped in the house. Mum and Dad will *kill* me when they get home, because there's nothing for tea and they'll be starving."

"What do you want me to do about it?" I tucked my hair behind my ear.

"If you can get rid of the ivy on the door, I'll clear the rest," said Dina. "There are pruners on the top of the log pile next to the shed."

I hesitated. Even though I had masked my smell and the drops had Nightmare Repellent, I had to be on my guard. If I slipped up and unleashed the Mother of All Nightmares, many lives would be in terrible danger.

"How do I know you are who you say you are? I mean, you could be anyone," I said. "Maybe you were trapped in there for a very good reason."

"I only want to put this mess right. If I don't, I'll be in trouble with my mum and dad, and then they'll squabble, and I'll have to go to bed and put a pillow over my head, so I don't have to listen to them bickering. *All night long.*"

I knew only too well what that was like, especially now Dad had lost his job.

"Tell you what, I'll pay you for your troubles," said Dina.

Having some extra money to give to Mum and Dad would be fantastic.

"How much?" I said.

"Two gold coins," she replied.

Cash Converters was around the corner from the Dream Store and its window was full of posters saying gold fetched a good price.

"Make it three gold coins, up front, and I'll do it," I said, folding my arms.

"How do I know you won't take the gold and run?" answered Dina.

"Do you see anyone else around willing to help?"

Dina sighed. "You drive a hard bargain, Ollo."

There was a rustling noise where the front door

must be and the tip of something round gleamed at the bottom of the ivy. I had to snatch the money from the clutches of the leaves before they could steal it from me. The coins were large, as golden as sunsets, and flashed in the light. I bit into one to test it wasn't made from chocolate and yelped when my tooth hit solid metal.

The money weighed heavy in my pocket.

Hurrying over to the log pile, I picked the pruners up.

I halted as Bert cried out my name in the distance.

There was a blood-curdling screech and a dragon flew overhead, its belly scraping against the tops of the trees.

A real, live, fire-breathing dragon. I rushed over to the cottage. I couldn't leave her, not with a dragon on the loose. If that were me, on my own, trapped inside, I'd be petrified. I snipped at the ivy with wild abandon. The surrounding leaves recoiled from the metal of the blade, but just as quickly the vines were growing back even thicker. Whatever was in the potion must have been strong.

"Ollo? If you cut the roots at the base of the door, it'll die back."

I hunkered down, my heart pounding like the drumbeat in a fast song. I felt my way to the base of the ivy and squeezed the cutters with all my might. As the vines were severed, the ivy leaves began to wither, changing the same colour as pickled onions.

I stepped back, scanning the sky for the dragon, but it was nowhere to be seen.

The door swung open with a loud creak as if it hadn't been opened in years.

A woman glided out of the cottage wearing a black crinoline dress with a sheen on it like the feathers on a raven. Through her lace veil I could see dark, sunken hollows where her eyes should have been. Her skin was as pale as moths and her red wine-gum-coloured lipstick was smudged around her mouth. I backed away from her, my eyes dropping to her skirt, which was made from black masks that had been stitched together. There was a gap at the front where one of the masks was missing.

"*You're Dina?*" I gasped.

"I'm Myrdina, the Mother of All Nightmares,

and I've been held prisoner in there for too long to mention," said the woman, in exactly the same girl's voice as Dina's. She tilted her head at me, like a crow trying to figure out a puzzle. "Children have been invisible to me, but for some reason, you're not. And another thing: not many could have cut through that ivy which was bound to the house by complex magic." She sniffed the air and I edged away from her.

Fear surged through me. The Nightmare Repellent mustn't be able to protect a Guardian of Dreamers. If she caught my scent, she'd know I could take her back to the real world. I stared at her, rooted to the spot.

"What are you waiting for, Ollo?" she said, sweetly. "A bad dream is no fun unless you're being hunted."

I kicked off my slippers, and fled.

Bert and Lantern burst through the trees, galloping towards me, sparks flying from the horse's hooves. I bolted across the grass, faster than I'd ever run away from Roxy Patterson. The knight circled around behind me, reached down and snatched me up.

I screamed at the top of my lungs and kicked my legs.

"Ollo, do not be afraid, you are safe! It is I, Bertrand Ponce de Leon!" boomed the knight.

I was flung to the side, where I landed, hard, on the saddle, wincing.

"Are you unharmed?" He pulled on the reins and squeezed Lantern's flanks so we turned towards the trees.

I threw my arms around the knight's middle. "Bert, am I glad to see you! That woman back there is the Mother of All Nightmares and she tricked me into releasing her. We need to get out of here."

"Did you say *the* Mother of All Nightmares?" asked the knight. "As in *the* Mother of All Nightmares?"

"Yes! Myrdina!"

"Why! This cannot be, for she does not exist in DreamDrops dreams!"

"She was imprisoned in the cottage, so you would never have known she was here!"

"This is grave news, indeed. And may I say, trouble seems to follow you wherever you go, Lady

Ollo." Bert cracked the reins and Lantern took off faster than the *Millennium Falcon*.

I plucked up the courage to check behind us.

Myrdina stood with her fists clenched at her sides. The mouths on the masks were moving and I could hear their whispers echoing all around.

The air became cold and damp. Tendrils of mist snaked down the embankment towards us, like grey octopus arms.

Lantern skidded to a halt and flattened his ears. Out of nowhere, a thick fog swirled in, making it impossible to see where we were going. The forest stilled, except for the stamping of Lantern's hooves and the creak of the leather saddle.

"Do you trust me, Lady Ollo?" said the knight, urgently.

"If it means never having to clap eyes on Myrdina again, I do," I said.

"Then hold on!" Clicking his tongue, he raised himself off the saddle and brandished the reins like whips.

Lantern reared and headed straight for the embankment.

The fog had veiled everything in a milky blanket, making it impossible to see a thing. Knotted trees loomed out of the mist only as we were inches away from them. I stifled my cries as their branches raked at my face and tugged at my hair. My heart leapt into my mouth as Lantern reached the top of the slope and galloped headlong into the fog, which had bleached everything white. I huddled down behind Bert, waiting for us to slam into a tree or for Lantern to stumble and fall.

I bit my lip so hard I tasted blood.

The mist curled in tendrils that streaked around the trees faster than arrows.

Something cold and burning coiled around my body, squeezing the breath out of me, dragging me off the horse.

"*Bert!*" I wheezed.

The knight glanced round. "It's the fog, Lady Ollo – I'll have to cut it off you."

There was the scrape of metal against metal and he drew his sword.

"Hold steady and when I say duck: *duck!*"

There was a rush of air and a flash of silver either

side of me, the mist exploding into shards of ice as it was spliced. He twirled the sword, swinging it low over the top of my head, clearing the last of it away.

"Now, *duck!*" he shouted.

A low branch flew out from nowhere and I dipped down just in time.

Bert hollered at Lantern, who sped up. We pulled ahead of the mist and tore through the woods. The wind roared in my ears and Lantern's hooves struck the ground, sending up a shower of sparks that were like orange fireworks against the grey of the fog. After what seemed like an eternity, we hurdled over a fallen tree trunk and came to a halt in a small clearing.

"Welcome to Camp de Leon, Lady Ollo." The knight jumped down from Lantern.

I slid off the horse, falling in a heap on the ground. "How did he not collide with any of the trees in that fog?" I asked.

"It's why I called him Lantern – this boy can navigate his way back home at night in the pitch dark." Bert led the horse over to a trough of water, where Lantern took a long drink. His sides shivered and the sweat made his coat shine like wet tar. The knight hurried over to me, sticking his hand out. I groaned as he hauled me to my feet.

"We don't have much time, Lady Ollo. The Mother of All Nightmares will use her magic to follow our tracks."

I peered through the trees nervously.

He led me to a den built from wood around the base of a tree and disappeared inside it.

I kicked my foot in the cold salt-and-pepper-coloured ashes of his campfire. "Shouldn't we be hiding from her or something?" I said.

"She's the Mother of All Nightmares – I don't have the magic necessary to keep us safe. We need to use what time we have wisely, and what you're about to learn could save your life if I'm unable to protect you," said a muffled voice from inside the den.

Bert reappeared with a sword and threw it over to me. It shot past me and thudded on the ground, sending a cloud of dust up. I bent down, coughing, and lifted it. The sword was gold with an ornate handle that had jewels embedded in it. It would surely fetch an impressive price at Cash Converters.

"It weighs a flippin' ton," I said.

The knight raced back into his den.

There was a rustling of leaves and the trees began to sway as if there was something enormous moving amongst them.

I let out a small whimper. A low grunt rumbled louder than thunder and a dragon poked its head out from between two oak trees. Its red eyes blazed and smoke wobbled out from its nostrils in perfect rings. The creature stepped into the clearing and shook itself, flapping its wings. Without taking my eyes off it for a second, I began to back away slowly, wishing I'd grabbed the sword to protect myself with.

"Bertttt ... *BERT!*" I whispered as loudly as I could.

The knight emerged and clocked the dragon. "Ah. I see you've met Firepuffles, then?"

I tripped over a stack of logs, landing on my backside. "Save. Me."

Bert laughed. "She's friendly, Lady Ollo. I'm sorry, I was not altogether truthful with you earlier on. We pretend to our customers that she's wild and ferocious, so that when they stand up to her they feel a real sense of achievement and grow in confidence – in complete safety."

I looked anxiously between Bert and the dragon, not convinced.

"Watch this." The knight picked up a stick and tossed it into the trees. A jet of flames exploded out from Firepuffles's mouth, which set fire to some washing Bert had out on a line. Firepuffles bounded after the stick, wagging her tail, and emerged seconds later with it between her jaws. After eating it, she thundered up to me to sniff my head. I held still, not daring to breathe. Firepuffles licked my face, covering it in slime, and trotted off to sit next to Lantern, who swished his tail.

I got to my feet, wiping my cheeks with my sleeve.

"Come, Lady Ollo, you must focus," said Bert, holding out a sword made from wood, which he handed to me. "Try that one for size."

The sword was strong and as light as a feather. I twirled it as if it was a baton. Bert also gave me a belt with a scabbard attached to it, which I slung around my waist.

"It's time for your lesson," Bert said.

He drew his sword out and circled around me, forcing me into the centre of the clearing, where the sun broke through the trees. It was hard to see him in the bright sunlight, and I brought my arm up to shield my eyes.

"Always take a good look at your surroundings and use what's around you to your advantage. If your opponent is blinded by the sunlight they won't be able to see you," he said.

The dragon snorted and I glanced at her, warily.

In one swift movement, the tip of his sword was suddenly a few millimetres away from my heart. "Eyes on your opponent. Don't ever become distracted. Never stand still, otherwise you're a sitting target, and always grip the sword with two hands because it'll give you more control."

I held the sword with both hands and kept moving. Bert lunged again and I nipped out of his way, keeping my sword raised.

"Good. Step away from your opponent's attack and block their sword as much as you can." The knight approached me and lunged with his sword.

I struck it away and moved forward, angling my sword at his chest.

"Not bad for a girl, Lady Ollo," he teased. "That's right, put all that anger into your sword and let your enemy feel the rage. At the same time, never let fury cloud your judgement. And remember, always try to use the element of surprise."

Leaves crackled and Lantern lifted his head, curling his upper lip as he scented the air.

Firepuffles leapt up, almost knocking Bert over with her tail. She slipped into the forest, her green scales making her invisible against the trees.

Bert swung round, his sword at the ready. I copied him.

The birdsong quietened and the air cooled.

A wall of fog flooded into the clearing through the trees. In an instant, I lost sight of Bert and Lantern.

The mist was damp against my skin, making me shiver. Every time a tendril curled around my arm or leg, I cut it away with the sword.

"Ollo! Stay where you are. I will find you!" shouted the knight. His voice sounded as if he was far away.

Something padded beside me in the mist, panting.

Sweat trickled down my back.

Long, low growling noises made goosebumps erupt over my skin. I sensed that I was surrounded. Whatever this was sounded much bigger than a dog.

Something howled in the distance.

A branch cracked and I swung in the direction of the noise, both hands on the handle of my sword.

There was an almighty snarl and the snapping of teeth.

I swallowed a scream and took off. Running blindly, I tripped over something on the forest floor and fell, knocking the wind out of my lungs. I dropped the sword and scrabbled around, frantically, until I clasped on to the wooden handle again.

I could hear Lantern's hooves on the ground and something else that was closer: the sound of lips being licked.

I struggled to my feet and stumbled forward. As I crept towards the sound of Lantern's hooves, the mist cleared in one enormous swirl. Myrdina stood with her veil rippling in the breeze, the masks on her dress grinning.

"I figured it out. Your perfume couldn't mask it, Ollo; the stench of you is unmistakable," she said. "You're a Guardian of Dreamers."

She shot towards me, grabbing hold of my wrist. Her nails dug into my skin and her veil scratched against my face.

"It's time for you to wake up, Ollo, and free me for good," said the Mother of All Nightmares.

I screamed at the top of my lungs.

CHAPTER 11

My heart kicked against my ribs. I leapt out of bed, flew across to the other side of the room, slammed into the wall and flicked on the light switch.

I was back home.

I checked every single one of the shadows for Myrdina. Only when I was sure she had been a dream did I let my breath out. I shuffled back to bed, falling face first on to the pillow with a groan.

My body hurt from head to toe and I was shattered.

Sitting bolt upright, I felt in my pocket for the gold coins.

They had gone!

I peeled back the duvet and patted around under it, but there was nothing. The coins must have been lost in Eldermere Forest. My toes struck something hard at the bottom of the bed. I reached down to find the wooden sword Bert had given me. I hoped the knight and Lantern were safe from Myrdina.

The bottle of DreamDrops gleamed on my bedside table. If all I'd brought back was a sword, then it had been worth having a dream, because with some practice, I could now defend myself against Roxy Patterson, be friends with Jeannie again and Mr Curley would never know what I'd been up to.

It was a win, win, win situation!

The end of my nose itched as everything in the room began to vibrate. I clutched my pillow, kneeling on my bed. The DreamDrops rattled, pens rolled off the desk, the ceiling light swung, the wardrobe creaked and the mirror fell off the wall, smashing into pieces.

There was a snapping and a whining noise. I peered over the edge of the bed as a pine tree burst through the floor. Its branches raked my face as it rose up towards the ceiling and through it. I flattened myself against the wall. Bits of plaster, dust, pine needles and small stones rained down, making me cough. More trees ruptured through the floor, which had grown a thick carpet of bright green moss covered in fallen leaves, twigs, cobwebs and mushrooms. A snake wound its way along a branch and something howled in the distance. The trees took on sinister shapes in the dim light and bats swooped through the branches, chasing insects.

My bedroom was now a forest! And not just any old forest; it was Eldermere Forest.

Everything Mr Curley had warned me about having a dream was coming true!

Something that sounded like two pan lids hitting off each other rattled inside my wardrobe.

I grabbed my sword, skirted around some mud and stood in front of the wardrobe. Wondering what it could be, I raised my sword, counted silently to three and flung the door open.

Huddled at the bottom of it was a boy knight.

I crouched down. *"Bert?"*

The knight had HP Sauce-coloured hair and a

freckle between his Slush Puppie–blue eyes.

"You found me! I knew you would!" I said. "Am I pleased to see you."

Bert scowled at me.

Then he slammed the door shut, nearly taking the tip of my nose off.

I knocked on the door. "Bert! It's me . . . Lady Ollo." Losing patience, I prised it open with my fingers.

"You're no lady!" he snapped. "Where am I?"

"You're inside a wardrobe."

He rolled his eyes. "I'd guessed that. Where is the wardrobe?"

"In my home."

Bert let out a cry. "Help a damsel in distress, I thought. How hard could it be? If I'd known you were a Guardian of Dreamers I would have done an about turn and galloped straight back into the woods. Not only have you unleashed the Mother of All Nightmares, but you then have the impudence to bring me and goodness knows what else back to your world." He lifted his head, his freckle puckering as he frowned. "I demand you put me back in A

Knight's Adventure. *NOW!*"

"Keep it down, Bert! I've got troubles of my own. I've no idea how I'm going to explain to Mum and Dad that my bedroom is now a flippin' forest."

"From where I'm sitting that's the least of your worries," said Bert, banging the door shut.

A deafening snort behind me made me freeze. The ground shuddered and the birds fell quiet. There was an almighty crash as a couple of trees fell over, narrowly missing me.

I spun around to see two red eyes glowing in the gloom. The dragon moved out from behind the trees, smoke trailing from its nose in oval rings. Firepuffles stretched her neck forward and blinked, her nostrils widening and narrowing as she sniffed the air. A throaty growl escaped from her mouth and her green scaly sides grew and shrank with every breath.

"Firepuffles!"

The dragon's eyes narrowed and her lip curled as she crouched.

"Bert!" I whispered out the side of my mouth. "There's something wrong with Firepuffles. She

doesn't seem to like me any more."

"Things from A Knight's Adventure don't act the same in this world. There's every chance Firepuffles is now highly dangerous."

I gulped. *"Let me in!"*

"Find your own hiding place. This one's taken," he hissed.

I lifted my sword with trembling hands and Firepuffles bared her teeth. I lowered it immediately. The dragon was so huge it would be like fighting it off with a cotton bud.

Firepuffles opened her mouth and a jet of scorching yellow flames shot out. I dived sideways on to my bed, the air filling with the scent of charred wood and hot pine resin. The dragon thundered towards me and I pressed my back against the wall, cowering behind my pillow. I peeped over the top of it to see the dragon towering over me.

The dragon's roar pinned me to the wall. Just as I was certain my time had come to an end, Firepuffles lifted her head, as though something above had caught her attention. Then she spread her wings, knocking another couple of trees over, and launched herself upwards, smashing straight through what was left of the ceiling. An avalanche of earth, grit and plaster hit me. As the dust settled, I caught a glimpse of Firepuffles disappearing off behind some pewter-coloured clouds.

I'd just released a dragon into Parradicehill. What had I done?

An urgent rap at the door made me jump.

"Ollo! What's going on? There's a strange mist out here and a swamp in the hallway," said Kyle.

"Leave me alone!" I yelled.

"I'm coming in!" Kyle pushed at the door, which was jammed shut by a clump of reeds.

I got down from the bed and ran across the forest floor, bounding over fallen trees. Just as I got to the door, Kyle crashed through it.

He whistled past me, knocking into a pine tree. He sat up, rubbing his forehead. His eyes widened to the size of biscuit tins as he took in the woods.

A pea-green bird zoomed past, screeching as it hunted a dragonfly.

"Ollo, whatever's going on, Mum and Dad are

going to kill you," he said.

"They'll need to get in line," I muttered, thinking about Roxy Patterson, Myrdina, Bert, Mr Curley and Firepuffles. "Can we keep this between ourselves until I can straighten things out? I'll do your dishes for the next month."

"Ollo, I wouldn't keep quiet about this even if you did my dishes for the rest of my life." Kyle watched in amazement as a stag bounded through the trees and disappeared.

A piercing scream came from somewhere in the flat.

Bert's armour started to rattle in the wardrobe.

Kyle and I rushed into the hallway, our feet squelching through thick, foul-smelling mud. The lights flickered and the wallpaper began to free itself from the walls, sheet by sheet.

We tore into the kitchen, skidding to a halt.

Mum stood, hand over her mouth. Next to her was a woman in a black dress wearing a lace veil. The paint on the ceiling cracked and fluttered down like spoiled cherry blossom petals. Mould bloomed around the window and cobwebs hung from the pulley like grey tights. A thin layer of mist bubbled up from the floor.

The Mother of All Nightmares was *in my house.*

She was even more terrifying now that she was standing in my kitchen. The place filled with the same smell of putrid rubbish from a bin on a hot day.

Just then, Dad hurried into the room.

"Who are you and how did you get into my home?" he growled at Myrdina.

She tilted her head, her lace veil scratching against her dress. The masks on her skirts watched but stayed tight-lipped.

"My name is Myrdina and I'm the Mother of All Nightmares. I'm here because your daughter had a dream and set me free."

"I don't care if you're Mother Teresa: my daughter can't dream, you're trespassing and I'm calling the police." Dad took his phone out of his pocket and as he dialled 999, the masks began to whisper. He juggled the mobile between his hands as if it was a hot potato and gasped as it started to drip the same way an ice lolly melts on a summer's day. The phone trickled through his fingers and ended up as a silver puddle on the floor.

He stared at Myrdina. "You owe me a new phone. I still had credit on that."

As long as the masks stayed silent, I knew we'd be safe.

"Dad – please, sit down!" I blurted out.

Myrdina ignored my dad, threw open the window and sniffed. "There is no fear in the air. Why are there so few children having nightmares in this place?"

"Where have you been, lady?" barked Kyle. "Trapped in a museum? Everyone is having good dreams because of Mr Curley's Dream Store."

All the glasses in the kitchen shattered, sending shards everywhere. Mum, Dad, Kyle and I ducked in fright.

Myrdina glided towards Kyle. Some eyes opened behind the masks; a tongue protruded from one of the mouths.

"Are you talking about Mr Tannis Curley?" she said, her bones creaking as she leaned forward.

"He makes stupid dreams that cost a fortune and sells them to kids so they don't have nightmares," said Kyle.

"That explains it." Myrdina returned to the window to peer down at the tiny houses and flats below. "I'll bet there's a child in each and every one of those homes. It's going to be glorious discovering what makes them whimper. I'll unleash their darkest fears and savour every delicious moment of their terror. And soon I won't just be a bad dream – I'll be real!" The masks on Myrdina's dress crackled.

Right at that moment, a dragon flew past the window, belching flames.

Myrdina clapped her hands together, in glee.

I wondered where Bert was. I'd seen his sword skills and they were impressive. Now would be a good time for the knight to launch an ambush against Myrdina.

Dad gathered himself. "Enough of this. Get out of my home!"

Myrdina focused her attention on him. "I've been locked away, unable to torment so much as a *slug*. I owe it to myself to have a bit of fun."

Dad scrabbled around the sink, found a mug

and hurled cold tea over her. A couple of the masks spluttered as the liquid streamed down her dress.

The masks started to hiss: a noise I'd not heard them make before.

"What did you do that for?" I wailed at him.

"It worked in *The Wizard of Oz*," Dad said, eyeing Myrdina nervously.

There was a puff of thick smoke and Dad was nowhere to be seen. The Mother of All Nightmares smiled. A fly buzzed around the room.

Had she just turned Dad into an insect?

One of the windows was open and the fly was dangerously close to it.

"Dad!" I shrieked as I dashed across the kitchen, leaned over the sink and slammed the window shut. I stopped to listen. I could no longer hear the buzzing noise.

What if he'd gone out the window?

As I scanned the room, I was relieved to spot a black fly sitting on a plate of half-eaten toast with raspberry jam.

"Where is my husband?" Mum grabbed a whisk and charged at the Mother of All Nightmares.

"No, Mum! Don't!" I shouted.

There was another almighty puff of smoke, which left Kyle and me coughing.

When it cleared, Mum had gone.

"What have you done with her?" I scanned the room. Dad was busy cleaning his wings on the plate, but he was the only fly I could see.

Myrdina laughed. "She's about to hug your dad. Isn't that lovely?"

A brown long-legged spider on the kitchen top crept up behind Dad with its jaws open, and he was too busy sucking up jam to notice. The spider pounced and Dad zipped away in the nick of time to settle on a dishcloth, where he wiped his eyes with his feet.

Mum was now a spider.

Myrdina appeared beside Kyle and me.

Gripping on to my shoulders, he pushed me towards her. "She's the worst sister ever. Be my guest. Turn her into anything you want."

"Kyle!" I said, shaking him off me and stumbling into the table.

Before I could do a thing, the Mother of All Nightmares stepped close to him and lifted her veil.

Kyle opened his mouth to scream but nothing came out. His eyes swivelled over to mine, full of fear. I watched in horror as his skin changed to the colour of stone. The grey spread down his neck like ink on tissue paper, covering his arms, legs and feet, until he became as solid as a brick wall.

Myrdina dropped her veil back down and shivered with delight. "Oh, that was good," she said. One of the masks on her dress flickered and lit up, glowing acid green.

I remembered what Mr Curley had said about Myrdina charging the masks with people's fear.

"Change him back or else!" I yelled.

"I don't think you're in a position to give orders, do you?" she said. Her hands cupped my face, her nails dug into my skin. "Besides, I've got something very special planned for you – and Mr Curley."

The Mother of All Nightmares vanished in a puff of screams which set the smoke alarm off. The noise was deafening and I daren't open the window in case Dad got out.

Swiping the dishcloth, I flapped it until the room cleared of smoke and the alarm stopped.

Out of the corner of my eye, I saw Mum scuttling towards the edge of the kitchen top.

I ran over to the recycling bag and found an empty jam jar and an envelope. Holding my breath steady, I approached Mum, who was crawling down the unit towards the floor. If she slipped underneath the counter, she could be lost for ever. Just as she landed on the tiles, I quickly put the jar on top of her, careful not to cut any of her legs off. I slid an envelope underneath the glass, lifted it up and placed it on the table. Mum scrabbled around the inside, trying to get out.

I whisked a piece of Peperami out of the fridge, put it on the chopping board and stepped back. It didn't take long before Dad noticed his favourite snack and zoomed over to it. I whacked an empty fruit punnet over him, weighing it down with a mug. He bumped around the sides of the tray and then settled on the sausage.

I walked over to Kyle. "If you can hear me, hang on in there. Mr Curley will know how to fix this." I patted his arm, which was as cold as concrete. The fact he couldn't say something rude back to me broke my heart. Kyle and I fought like cat and dog, but it didn't mean to say I didn't love him. He didn't deserve this.

Mr Curley had been right. So had Seraphina. I had made things so much worse. And on top of everything else, the gallant knight had been a no-show.

I fled to my room, stomped past the trees, swerved a badger, marched up to the wardrobe and flung the door open.

"The Mother of All Nightmares is here. My mum has eight legs because she's a spider and she just tried to eat my dad, who's a fly; my brother has been turned into a statue; and there's a dragon on the loose. Where were *you*?"

"Ollo, the clue is in the name. You released the Mother of All Nightmares. What else did you expect?" he replied.

I grasped on to his tunic and hauled him out of the wardrobe. "Do you have any words of wisdom on how I can get my mum, dad and brother back to normal?"

Bert looked the other way.

"You're a knight. You made an oath. You're honourable and brave. You fight like a legend. You save damsels in distress. And you swore on your life you'd help."

He edged away from me, accidentally brushed against a holly bush and squealed. "Everything in this place is dangerous and scary and, quite frankly, detestable. In A Knight's Adventure I have unlimited lives – I can be as chivalrous and foolhardy as I please with no consequences. But here I've only got one life, and I'm going to be doing my very best to keep myself alive at all cost. This is your mess; you deal with it."

"But what about your house motto: potty qwammy-something or other?"

"It doesn't apply here. Read my lips: this knight is off duty."

I scowled at Bert. He was about as courageous as a lump of plasticine. But without him I was done for.

He staggered past a stagnant stream, over to the window, where he did a double take at the view.

"Do you live in the clouds, Ollo?" he asked.

"This is a high-rise, the tallest building in Parradicehill, and we're on the top floor, so that's why it feels as though we're in the heavens." I glanced out the window and spied a plume of smoke rising in the distance. "Oh no!"

Bert's armour rattled as he hid behind a pine tree. "W-what now?"

"I think the Dream Store is on fire, and I'll bet you Myrdina has something to do with it."

Mr Curley was going to be furious with me. For so many reasons . . .

"You go," said Bert, steering me through the trees towards the door before giving me a final shove. "I'll stay and be your lookout." He made his way straight to the wardrobe and climbed back inside it.

"Bert!" I roared. "Mr Curley's in trouble!"

The knight pushed the door ajar. "And that's my problem because . . .?"

I wracked my brain to think of something I could say that might get through to him.

"If you hate this world so much, you're going to want to go home," I said at last. "Right?"

He nodded. "I'd do anything to be at my camp in the forest, gutting fish, tending the fire and sharpening my swords."

"Mr Curley makes the dreams. He's the only one who can get you home to A Knight's Adventure, but not if his store is destroyed by Myrdina. Help him, and he's your ticket back to the world you dearly love."

The knight sighed. Then he crawled out of the wardrobe. "This was definitely not in my contract," he muttered.

I grabbed my DreamDrops off the forest floor. The drops no longer rattled; they sloshed about inside the bottle as though they'd melted. Perhaps Mr Curley would know what was wrong with them? I shoved the bottle in my rucksack and raced to the hall cupboard, where I threw on my trainers and zipped up my coat. I opened the front door.

"Come on, Bert!" I yelled.

Bert dragged his heels down the hallway, his shoulders slumped. "Is it far?" he said.

"About a twenty-minute walk. Quicker if we run."

"Have you tried jogging in armour?" He pulled a face. "We should take Lantern."

"He's here?" I said, astonished.

The knight tipped his head in the direction of

the lounge.

I bolted into the room. The horse snorted and flicked his tail, knocking over a lamp that smashed. He was nibbling on the straw-coloured tassels of a cushion and there was a giant pile of poop on the rug, something Dad would probably be very happy about now that he was a fly.

I scratched behind Lantern's ears as he chewed on my coat sleeve.

"I'm so glad you're here. Come on, let's get going," I said, taking the reins and leading Lantern out of the front door and along the landing to the lift. The knight followed us, mumbling rude words behind his shield.

When the lift arrived and the doors pinged open, there was an old lady inside, who clutched her handbag to her chest as the knight, the horse and I squeezed in beside her.

CHAPTER 12

Clouds gathered in the sky, robbing the town of all of its colour. The air cooled and a breeze agitated the trees.

Not wanting to draw more attention to ourselves than was necessary, we avoided the main streets and stole through people's gardens, jumping over fences and hedges. Although Lantern looked the same, sparks no longer flew from his hooves and he was slower than he'd been in A Knight's Adventure.

We reached the Dream Store without bumping into Myrdina, Roxy Patterson or the dragon.

As we approached, I drew in my breath. The window was cracked and the spacewoman, her rocket and the planets had disappeared. I stepped inside, my trainers crunching over an intricate mosaic of smashed glass and slimy drops.

Myrdina must have used her magic to destroy all the DreamDrops!

Mould grew around the windows and spiderwebs were draped on the shelves and plinths like grey bunting. There was no aroma of sweets, cakes or chocolate: only acrid smoke. The sense of excitement and adventure that filled every corner of the Dream Store was gone.

A noise in the basement made my head snap up.

Could it be Mr Curley?

Bert crashed through the door and I leapt out of my skin.

"Tethered Lantern next to a patch of grass. At least one of us is happy," he said.

I put my fingers to my lips and tiptoed over to the green curtains. Bert followed me, his armour clanking.

"Keep it down, tin head!" I hissed. "There's someone downstairs."

He replied with something I'm not sure knights are strictly allowed to say under oath.

I crept down the spiral staircase, pausing halfway to listen out. Silence.

Bert whimpered. Cursing that I'd been stuck with such a useless heap of scrap metal, I snuck into the basement. The walls were cracked and Mr Curley's possessions were strewn everywhere. I stepped over ripped pages of books, shredded cushions and pieces of statue. A thin mist swirled around my feet.

I could hear a banging noise. And it was coming from a cupboard under some shelves. Bert ducked behind a cabinet.

I crouched, my heart in my mouth, and drew my sword as I reached for the handle. I wrenched it open and something black zoomed straight into my face.

Crying out, I fell backwards.

The bird circled the room and dive-bombed me, wailing like a burglar alarm.

It was Sausage!

And she was furious. I covered my head with my hands as she pecked at my fingers. I struggled to my feet.

Sausage landed beside me on the leg of an overturned chair. I stared past her and my heart stopped.

The large mirror had been smashed, exposing the secret room behind it. I gripped my sword hard, summoning up the courage to go inside.

It was dark as I entered, but I could just make out a large hole in the bricks, where the window had been. The Book of Nightmares had gone. I lifted up the blind on the top of the box to discover the mask was no longer there either.

If Myrdina had the mask it meant that there was nothing to stop her from becoming real. All she had to do was scare enough children.

I wondered what else she had taken. Surely not . . .

"Oh no!" I said. "The Book of Dreams!"

Sausage searched frantically for the painting of the wolfhound. After checking under cushions, newspapers, rugs and piles of books, I found it wrapped in a map of the world. Sausage pecked at the wolfhound's nose and the Persian rug on the wall slid to the side.

I ran to the door and entered, with my sword raised, almost too afraid to look. I breathed out a sigh of relief as soon as I saw the book glowing under the spotlight. The sight of it was so beautiful and reassuring, you could almost forget the Mother of All Nightmares was on the loose.

I gazed at the pages and noticed they weren't turning.

There had been no new dreams recorded since yesterday.

"Where is Mr Curley, Sausage?" I asked the bird, but she glided towards the courtyard without even glancing my way.

"Ollo!" shouted Bert.

I ran outside and gasped. The Dream Factory had been reduced to a smouldering pile of rubble. Myrdina had made sure Mr Curley would not be able to make any more DreamDrops.

Bert was standing with his shield up and his sword drawn, edging closer to something under the tree.

I followed his gaze and saw that it was Mr Curley, crouching down, grey from head to toe, just like Kyle. His hands were clamped to his face, his fingers fanned out across his cheeks. His eyes and mouth were wide open in horror.

Bert lowered his shield and poked at Mr Curley with his sword. Cracks snaked all around his body like a network of black veins. His head rolled off to the side and he collapsed, disintegrating into a heap of dust right in front of us.

"What did you do that for?" I wailed, falling to my knees.

"I hardly touched him," protested Bert.

Without Mr Curley, how could we stop Myrdina? And how was I going to save my mum, dad and brother?

Sausage landed on the grass. Miserable, she scratched through the dirt.

I scooped up a handful of dust in an attempt to put him back together, but his remains sifted through my hands like sugar.

This was all my fault.

"I'm so sorry, Sausage," I said.

The bird opened her wings, spread her tail feathers and hissed at me.

Bert backed away.

"Sausage, if I'd known this was going to happen to Mr Curley, or that my family would suffer, I never would have stolen the drops."

The bird stayed silent, which made me feel worse. Sausage flapped on to a low stone wall.

I took a deep breath and tried to focus, the same way I had when I'd made the Pirate Arrrrdventure essence. Sausage and Bert watched as I paced up and down deep in thought. Mr Curley had imprisoned Myrdina within a dream. Perhaps there was still time for me to do the same . . .

"I'm not asking you to like me – but if I'm to make this right, you'll need to hear me out. You know the Mother of All Nightmares wants to become real?"

Sausage shook herself and Bert's armour rattled like a bin rolling down a hill as he glanced around warily.

"Myrdina has used her magic to destroy all the drops, and not just in the store." I took out my own bottle of DreamDrops. A liquid moved around sluggishly inside. "I had this one at home and it's ruined too. What if everyone's drops are like this? Without them, kids will no longer be protected against her. The Book of Dreams hasn't recorded a single good dream today, which means she is getting stronger. If there's one thing I know about Mr Curley, it's that he'd do anything to keep children safe from the Mother of All Nightmares – even if that means having to trust me when I've done nothing to earn it." I wiped my nose on my sleeve. "Mr Curley loved my ideas for dreams and I think he taught me enough for me to make one on my own. If I can come up with a way to imprison Myrdina, just like Mr Curley did in A Knight's Adventure, then there's a chance I might be able to trap her in the dream world." My eyes flicked over to what remained of Mr Curley. "I was the one who released her; let me be the one to capture her."

Sausage avoided my gaze.

"It wasn't Myrdina who shut you in the cupboard, was it?" I said. "It was Mr Curley."

The bird preened the feathers on her wings.

"He did it because he wanted you to be safe. Let's see if we can keep the children here safe too. We have to try, Sausage. But we don't have long – a few hours at most."

"Knickers," muttered the bird. She took off, corkscrewed over to the Dream HQ and said her name, which opened the door.

"Come on, Bert, I think we just got the green light." I hurried along the path towards Dream HQ.

"Whoop-de-doo," said the knight gloomily as he clanked after me.

Although the building was still standing, the ceiling had been smashed and thousands of shark-fin-shaped pieces of glass glittered on the blue tiled floor. The drawers had been mangled beyond recognition and the workbench had been reduced to a pile of firewood.

"What is this place?" asked Bert, his foot jabbing at a plant no longer in its pot.

"Mr Curley made all the dreams here," I replied. "I had one of the best days ever helping him create Pirate Arrrrdventure essence. All I had to do was imagine what would be in the dream and the magic ingredients appeared inside the drawers. But look at them. They're ruined. I'm not so sure I can do this after all."

It was strange being in Dream HQ without Mr

Curley. What had I been thinking that I could be like him? That I'd be able to catch Myrdina using magic I'd only just learned? My eyes welled up.

A battered purple drawer that lay on its side opened up a crack. I wormed my fingers through the gap, and after a few goes, managed to pull out one of Mr Curley's handkerchiefs. I remembered him saying that Dream HQ always knew what you needed. I bawled into the hanky.

I'd made such a mess of everything. Myrdina would be unstoppable now.

Sausage flew over and pecked me on the leg.

"Ow!" I said, sniffing. "What was that for?"

Bert laughed. "I suspect she's telling you to pull yourself together."

Sausage settled on a plank of wood and strutted along it. "Dream HQ – *fix*," said the bird, perfectly mimicking Mr Curley's voice.

My eyes filled up at hearing it again. I blew my nose and dabbed the tears away.

A shard of glass next to my foot trembled and shot towards the ceiling. Bert jumped.

We watched as, one by one, the pieces of glass rose

up high, each one flashing like a diamond before they snapped neatly back together, until the entire ceiling was once again complete. Bert leapt out of the way as some of the drawers righted themselves, pushing out their dents, sealing up the cracks and smoothing the twists and bends in them. The workbench reassembled itself, nails flying up from the floor to secure its broken sections of wood back together. An armchair flipped on to its feet, its stuffing swarming across the floor towards it in white puffs. Pictures reattached themselves to walls, plants and spilled earth bounced back into their pots, and rugs crawled like caterpillars to their places on the floor.

Everything was back in order. Now it was up to me.

When I had been unsure of how to make Pirate Arrrrdventure essence, Mr Curley had told me to *just give it a whirl.*

I took a huge breath. "Can I have a bottle, please, Dream HQ?" I said. The drawers stayed firmly shut.

I tried again. "Excuse me, Dream HQ – would you be able to give me a mixing bottle? I need to try and make an essence."

Not even Bert moved.

Mum worked as a secretary and told me she sometimes stood like a superhero in the stationery cupboard so she'd feel more confident. I positioned my feet slightly apart, placed my hands on my hips and tilted my head upwards.

Sausage eyeballed me.

"Dream HQ! A bottle for the essence I'm going to capture the Mother of All Nightmares with! This instant!"

A small pine drawer opened, its handle falling off and rolling across the floor. Inside was an empty blue bottle and some glue, which I presumed must be for the handle. I grinned triumphantly, took them out and placed them on the bench.

My smile wavered.

I had only made one other dream essence – what if I couldn't do it again?

"How am I going to trap her?" I said, out loud.

Bert stepped forward. "What you want is to construct a castle with high walls, impenetrable defences, a moat and a dungeon. That way she'll never be able to escape."

I shook my head. "Kids love castles, Bert. They're like adventure playgrounds for children. I have to create something that they'd never go near in a million years."

Bert pondered this, drumming his fingers on the worktop. "How about a *haunted* castle, then?"

"That's even more of a magnet for kids. What is it with you and castles?"

He rolled his eyes. "Duh, I'm a knight."

"Could have fooled me," I said under my breath. "Well, what do you suggest?"

I raised my eyes to the skies and watched as clouds raced past, each one eager to be the first to touch the sun. All of a sudden, an idea came to me. I thought for a minute and then I began writing.

Bert and Sausage stayed quiet until I had finished. I checked over the list, until I was certain I had everything I needed. "Do you think you could make yourself useful and collect the ingredients from the drawers?"

"Must I?" said Bert.

"It'll mean I can work twice as fast."

Sausage strutted up and down, watching me coolly.

I cleared my throat and began to read the ingredients out aloud.

I heard the swoosh and rattle of drawers opening and closing, and Bert sighing as he collected the ingredients.

"What are Fang Granules for?" asked the knight, taking the lid off the tub and sticking his nose into the powder.

"Careful, tin head – these ingredients can be dangerous," I warned.

The knight replaced the lid and plonked the container on the bench. Just then there was a popping noise and Bert doubled over in agony, clutching his mouth. When he straightened up and took his hand away, his front teeth had grown so huge they protruded out all the way down to his chin.

"Whath hath you thon tho me?" Bert strode over to a mirror and shrieked. "I wath handthome unthil you broth me here, againth my will."

Sausage hid her head under her wing.

"You've only had a tiny amount," I said reassuringly. "You'll return to normal soon – and if not, look on the bright side: tough steak will never be a problem for you again."

I checked the labels on each container, noticing that there were a few I hadn't asked for, like Balloon Bubbles, Breeze Brew and Dinghy Sprinkles. Maybe Dream HQ hadn't completely recovered yet.

I lined up all the ingredients and measured them out exactly the same way Mr Curley had shown me. Even though I trembled, I managed not to spill a drop. I blast chilled the contents that were active and then ran through my list again to discover Lightning Spark was missing.

"Lightning Spark," I called out to the room. I heard a thump. Checking the drawers, I could see one had been so badly damaged it had jammed. I took my sword out and wedged it into the gap, levering it forward until there was a splitting noise. As I eased the drawer fully open there was a blinding flash, and lightning streaked past me to strike the wall opposite, leaving a blackened hole that smoke poured out of.

Sausage flung herself on to the floor, where she hid behind a plant.

The knight ducked under the workbench. *"You're worth than Firepuffleth."*

The air crackled. The hair on my arms and on the back of my neck stood on end.

There was another burst of lightning, which forked above my head, hitting some metal lights that exploded, sending yellow sparks everywhere. I bombed over to the chair, snatched Bert's shield and raised it in front of me as I charged back to the drawer.

The Lightning Spark bottle must have been chipped when Myrdina was trying to destroy the place.

There was an almighty flash and Bert cried out as lightning struck his armour.

I pounced on the bottle, winding the hanky around it like a tourniquet. Moving swiftly, I thrust it inside the blast chiller.

Bert collapsed into the chair, wisps of smoke rising from him.

The damaged bottle couldn't go back in the drawer, so after I chipped off some flakes into the essence, I lobbed it out the window. The courtyard strobed as the lightning zapped around the garden, upsetting the birds and scorching branches.

Sausage came out from behind the plant, her feathers ruffled.

I smoothed my hair down and ploughed on. Eventually there was only one other ingredient left to add.

"Nightmare Repellent," I called out to the room.

A thin metal drawer opened next to the knight, which he refused to touch. I collected the container and added a drop of the potion into the mix, stirring the contents. The liquid fizzed violently and then glided around the bottle in white and grey streaks, constantly changing shapes, smelling of the air in summer before a storm breaks. I knew from what Mr Curley had told me that the essence would be strong. All I needed was for Myrdina to take one tiny drop, and if I'd done my job right, she'd be returned to the dream world, where she'd once again be imprisoned.

"Are you finithed?" asked Bert.

"I think I've done everything I need to," I said. "Now all we have to do is find Myrdina."

"Seriouthly?" said Bert, as one of his eyes twitched.

Sausage flew past us, out into the courtyard, where she dodged the last bolt of lightning.

I tightened the top of the bottle and placed the dream essence in my rucksack. As we went out, a small violet drawer with flowers on it opened by the door. There was a torch inside. *It must be a mistake*, I thought, but I shoved it in my rucksack anyway.

We zoomed across the courtyard, up the stairs and through the store to find Lantern with his nose pressed against the window. I changed the open sign to closed on the door. Bert wasn't as agile as he'd been in A Knight's Adventure. It took him three attempts to climb on to the horse.

Sausage circled overhead, ticking like a clock, impatient to get going.

I waited for Bert to reach down and help me up, but he didn't. I sighed, dragged a blue recycling bin over, heaved myself on to it, wobbled and flung myself over Lantern, who bucked.

"Where are we off to?" asked Bert, running his

tongue across his teeth, which had shrunk back to normal.

"Myrdina will be looking for children to terrorize. We should check the Goldburn Shopping Centre first," I said thoughtfully. "There's a cinema and a lot of kids go there on a Saturday morning."

"Which direction is it?" asked Bert.

"That way," I said, pointing to the right.

Bert quickly steered Lantern to the left, and nudged him into a trot.

I tapped him on the shoulder. "You're going the wrong way!" I said.

"If you think I'm venturing anywhere near the Mother of All Nightmares, you can think again. I saw what she did to your brother and Mr Curley. I don't want to end up as a lump of rock. Or a spider. Or a fly, thank you very much. I want to get back to A Knight's Adventure in one piece. You and that angry bird are on your own."

Sausage swooped at us, blowing raspberries.

I rolled my eyes. "Have you really not figured it out yet? With Mr Curley gone, who do you think is going to get you back home now?"

Bert tilted his head forward and made a noise like a wounded animal. "Don't tell me it's you? Oh, the gods have been very, very, very cruel to me."

"They have, Bert. Now can we go in the right direction? Because we really don't have any time to lose."

CHAPTER 13

Goldburn Shopping Centre was where Jeannie and I would hang out after school if the weather was bad. It was on two levels and filled with boutiques, gift stores, empty units, and stalls selling stuff you'd never want to buy.

We tethered Lantern in the deserted lane down the side of the building and made our way inside, Sausage perching on Bert's shoulder.

There was always someone dressed up doing promotions on the concourse, so nobody batted an eyelid at the knight, though I drew a few glances for being in my pyjamas. We marched up the escalator, keeping our eyes peeled for a woman in black. The thought of coming face to face with Myrdina again made my nerves skip like stones across the water.

My trainers squeaked as I raced along the floor. I stopped outside Snowflakes Ice Cream Parlour. It was a favourite hangout in Parradicehill because it looked like an old 1950s diner and even had a jukebox. Jeannie and I used to come here as a treat to share a sundae.

There were loads of kids around, and to my relief none of them seemed to have been turned to stone.

Bert's eyes widened as he watched children tucking into towering scoops of every-flavour-imaginable ice cream.

"Can we go in?" he asked, licking his lips.

A table of girls got up to leave, and that's when I saw them. Jeannie was sharing our favourite sundae with Roxy Patterson. I watched as they laughed behind their hands, their spoons digging into Sour Cherry, Banana Splitz and Fudge-a-Rama with extra chocolate sauce.

My heart felt as though it had been stamped on.

I steadied my breath. I had much bigger things to worry about than them. With Myrdina roaming around, no child was safe.

"We'll try the cinema," I said firmly. "*Chilled 3* is on and everyone at school was talking about going to see it." I dragged the knight away from the shop and we sped off, only slowing to stroll past a security guard.

We cut through a seating area that was overgrown with plastic ferns and bombed into the foyer of the cinema, the smell of sweet and salty popcorn and cheesy nachos filling our noses. The place was empty, but that was because the film had already begun.

"Come on – nobody will notice if we slip inside for a quick look around," I said.

Dramatic music rumbled in the background as we stole past the deserted ticket office and nipped down a dimly lit corridor, which had a worn blood-red swirly patterned carpet. Sausage huddled on Bert's shoulder. She pecked him when the knight became distracted by a film poster that had a picture of a castle on it. I opened the door to cinema one and we tiptoed along a narrow aisle, the music drowning out the clank of Bert's armour. I peered round the corner. I could see from all the silhouettes that the cinema was busy, but it was too dark for me to make anything out. Bert, amazed by the big screen and moving pictures, wandered out to stand in front of it, not believing his eyes.

All of a sudden, the cinema screen brightened up, illuminating the crowd. That's when I realized: everyone's faces were grey and frozen in screams. A thin mist swirled around their feet and cobwebs hung from the arms of the red velvet chairs as though the material had aged and torn. Black paint chips flaked off the walls, drifting down like ash from a bonfire.

I staggered backwards, feeling sick to the pit of my stomach.

What if I can't put this right? I wondered. *What if they're stuck like this for ever?*

The screen lit up again and I saw Myrdina gliding behind the seats right at the back.

All the masks on her skirts were black, except for the row around her waistband, which glowed a ghoulish green.

"Wait!" I cried out. "You can't do this!"

"I'm only just getting started, Ollo. And as soon as I become real – it'll be too late for them, Mr Curley and your family." Myrdina chuckled and gave me a big wave before she vanished into thin air.

If I wanted to save all these lives, I was going to have to catch the Mother of All Nightmares, because she was well on her way to becoming real. There was a Go Wild Safari indoor adventure centre along from here. It would be teeming with children, and if I was Myrdina, that's where I'd head to next.

"Sausage! I think I might know where Myrdina is!" I yelled over the music.

The bird spun into a dive and landed on Bert's shoulder, making him shriek.

We sprinted out of the cinema, along to Go Wild Safari. I'd not been there in years. Kyle and I used to go all the time until it became uncool for him to hang out with me.

Large plastic flamingos guarded either side of the entranceway. Bert stopped and drew his sword.

"Oh, come on, they're not real," I snapped, dragging him inside. Then I halted.

Usually Go Wild Safari was full of kids running around, shouting. But today it was deathly silent. There was a thin mist on the ground and cobwebs hung from the walls.

I only hoped we weren't too late.

To our right, the café lay empty: mugs and glasses still on the tables. Straight ahead was the adventure play area, which was ideal for children wanting to have fun, but not so great for catching the Mother of All Nightmares.

I didn't have time to be afraid. I shook all bad thoughts from my head, fished out the dream essence from my rucksack and stuck it in my pocket. I slung my bag over my back and tightened the belt holding my sword.

"If either of you spot Myrdina, don't make a sound, otherwise you could be in danger."

Sausage didn't look at me, but I could tell she was listening.

I pelted forward and bounded up some padded steps encased in safety netting. This was the way to the tower. Sausage took to the air and the knight followed me, trying his best not to rattle too much.

I felt sick at the thought of being up so high, but at the top, we'd get a good view of the whole play area and hopefully spy Myrdina.

Even though I felt queasy, I tore up three flights of stairs, and didn't bat an eyelid at the plastic crocodile that snapped its jaws or the snakes that hung down in coils from the ceiling. I gripped on tightly to the handrails and staggered over a V-shaped rope walkway that rocked from side to side. Stepping off it, I got down on my hands and knees and squeezed myself through a narrow orange tunnel. Something swung across my path, and I yelled out, then gasped in relief. It was just a mechanical monkey. Not Myrdina.

There was a clatter behind me and I glanced back through the tunnel to see Bert scarpering from the crocodile.

"It's not real, Bert!" I shouted, but he'd gone. There was no time to go after him; I had to catch Myrdina. I flung myself into a green tunnel and shuffled forward towards a giant slide, which I whizzed down, landing in a pit filled with hundreds of brightly coloured balls. The balls shifted, exposing two grey faces next to me that were fixed in screams. I swallowed a yell, and backed away from the boys in fright. Mist started to tumble in over the edges of the pit.

Myrdina must have just been here!

Up above, a movement caught my eye and I saw a black figure crouch down, then slip silently into a red tunnel. Seconds later I heard screams coming from it.

Without making a peep, Sausage began tracking Myrdina from a distance. The Mother of All Nightmares was heading for the heart of the play area where the trampolines were.

After spending hours here with Kyle, I knew that if I could reach the walkway above the trampolines, there were Nerf Blasters. I could attract Myrdina's attention – and that would be my chance to trap her with the dream essence.

I tore down the corridor and leapt on to an abandoned scooter. Gathering speed, I whizzed around the corner, past a hippo, to the stairway. A girl was halfway up, petrified solid, stone tears on her cheeks. Storming up the last of the steps,

I dashed towards the Nerf Blasters, grabbed one, then edged towards the parapet. I could see Sausage, circling frantically. Below her, the Mother of All Nightmares was approaching four kids who were bouncing around on the trampolines.

I raised the Nerf Blaster, took aim and fired at Myrdina, hitting her with a round of foam darts. She cursed so loudly, the kids clocked her, bounded off the trampolines and ran for their lives towards the exit.

I fired another round.

The Mother of All Nightmares lifted up her head and stared in my direction.

I froze.

The mouths on the masks moved; whispers and chants echoed around the slides and walkways, and the lights flickered and went out, plunging the place into darkness.

Strange cries, roars and grunts filled my ears.

The walls were decorated with luminous paint, so it was still possible to make out some shapes and outlines. Leaning over the barrier, I steadied myself, and scanned below for Myrdina.

Emergency lighting flickered on, casting the place in an eerie glow.

The air cooled and something scratched against the back of my neck.

I whirled around and shreiked in horror. Seeing her up close never got easier.

My eyes flicked to Myrdina's skirts.

Another row of masks were glowing radioactive green.

"You Guardians of Dreamers are such a bunch of killjoys, trying to save the kids," she said. "I'm bored with this place; the young ones aren't much fun, they scare too easily. I fancy a change of scene. Perhaps there's a nice park nearby? Too bad you won't make it along."

Myrdina shoved me with so much strength that I broke through the safety netting and fell. I closed my eyes and flailed my arms. Hitting the floor from this height would crush every bone in my body. As I landed, all the air was punched out of my lungs. Dazed, I raised my head to see a blue crash mat had been moved to cushion my fall.

In the gloom, I caught the glint of a silver shield.

"Thanks, Bert," I croaked.

"You can't very well get me back to Eldermere Forest if you're dead, can you? And on that note, I'd move it if I were you. You have company."

Something gave a deafening grunt and I scrambled to my feet.

A fibreglass hippo charged towards me, its jaws open.

I screamed.

Myrdina had brought the model animals to life!

The knight and I ran towards a rope swing. Underneath, the safety net was covered in writhing snakes. We both grabbed on to the ropes and jumped to escape the hippo. I used the momentum to swing myself forward and catch the next rope. As I glided over the snakes, their heads darted upwards. My body had never felt so heavy and my fingers found it hard to get a grip. I grasped on to the last section of rope, flew through the air and landed on the platform, where I did a wobble at the edge, before I straightened up.

The hippo stamped its feet and flapped its ears, its tiny eyes gleaming.

Bert was on the second rope, but his heavy

armour was making it impossible for him to follow me. I watched in dismay as he began to slip lower, inching nearer to the snakes.

I held on to the rope, pushed hard off the platform and swung back out, gaining height.

"Hold on, Bert!" As I neared him, I hooked my arms around his rope and rocked it backwards and forwards until he was once again swinging. Zipping through the air, I landed back on the platform, only to be knocked over like a skittle by the knight.

Sausage trumpeted and landed on his shoulder.

We picked ourselves up and snuck forward towards the entrance.

I stuck my head out and checked the ticket office.

There was the tinkle of glass smashing, and my head whipped round towards the café. A gorilla was behind the counter, helping himself to the cakes and sandwiches.

Careful not to make a sound, Bert and I tiptoed as quietly as we could past the ape.

Just as I thought we were safe, the knight dropped his shield, which clattered to the floor and spun in circles.

"Knickers," said Sausage, taking off.

The gorilla climbed on to the counter, striking its chest with its fists. Sausage hovered above the ape to distract it.

Bert snatched up his shield and I pulled him out of Go Wild Safari. When Sausage finally appeared, I slammed the door firmly shut behind us. As we fled, we startled the two pink flamingos in the doorway. They took off towards the shops, where we heard the shouts of the security guard as he tried to catch them.

With no time to lose, even Bert ran like the wind to fetch Lantern.

CHAPTER 14

"*This* is your park? It looks like it has been cursed by a wicked queen."

Bert took off his helmet and gawped, astonished at the stairsteps, vert ramps, quarter pipes and spine transfers.

"This is the *skate park*," I said. I didn't have time to explain skateboarding to the knight. "The children's playground is around the corner. If we sneak up on Myrdina, we'll have a better chance of catching her."

"What do you mean *we*?" said Bert.

"Fine," I said. "Sausage and I will go."

The bird shook herself as she perched on the branch above us.

Bert shrugged and glanced away. "Lantern and I will wait here. Try not to get turned into a garden ornament."

I scowled at him and set off, keeping well hidden behind the trees lining the play area.

Sausage followed me at a distance.

The wind poked the branches, making them clack and creak; the leaves clung on to their stems, fluttering like small green flags. The sky darkened as if a storm was brewing.

My stomach knotted. It was awful that I had caused this. And if I couldn't stop Myrdina, then things would only get worse.

I reached into my pocket and my fingers felt the comforting coolness of the dream essence bottle. I just had to get close enough so I could put one drop in Myrdina's mouth.

I jogged along the line of trees, glimpsing figures in the playground through the branches. Flattening myself against the last trunk, I peeped around the side of it. A girl was on the swings, her toes pointed as she flew through the air. Next to her was a climbing frame and a roundabout.

Sausage watched me from a branch, her head bobbing up and down.

I edged my way closer. Some toadstools and weeds had pushed their way up through the rubber matting and it was squishy underfoot. As I crept up to the swings, the girl swung towards me: her face was grey and her mouth stretched wide open. I staggered back, knocking into a boy hanging by his hands off the climbing frame. The look of terror etched on his stone face chilled me to the bone. The roundabout beside the climbing frame squeaked to a halt, every child on it as grey as roof tiles. On the benches, people sat frozen like creepy sculptures.

Wisps of mist began to drift over the edge of the playground.

I whirled around to see Myrdina standing on the grass, eyeballing me. Dead leaves fluttered down around her and a stone squirrel fell from the trees, landing at her feet with a thump.

I squinted my eyes. Myrdina only had three more rows of masks left to light up on her skirts.

I started towards her. She shrieked with laugher. "Ollo! The best is yet to come," she said before she vanished.

Breaking into a run, I shot through the trees. Sausage darted through the waving branches with the precision of a fighter jet.

Bert was sitting on Lantern, his shield raised and his sword at the ready. "Is it Myrdina? Is she here?"

"She's very close to becoming real! We have to stop her before it's too late!" I said.

The knight put away his sword and lowered his shield. He cleared his throat. "It's freezing out here, Ollo. My armour weighs a ton and chafes in places you wouldn't believe. I've been on the go all day, without a single thing to eat, and my skull feels as if I have an axe embedded in it. Lantern's exhausted – neither of us are getting any younger."

"Spit it out, Bert," I said, through gritted teeth.

"Look, even if you went to every single park or swimming pool or sweet shop in this dreadful town, I doubt you'd catch her because she appears to be one step ahead of you. A word of advice from an ex-knight: put a solid plan of action together, or you'll end up failing your quest."

There was some truth to what he was saying, which made me even more annoyed. I booted a stone and watched as it skipped across the path. If I knew for sure where the Mother of All Nightmares was going to appear next, I'd have a better chance of capturing her, otherwise I could end up going round and round in circles, always too late, while Myrdina was growing stronger.

Sausage swooped low over our heads, blaring like a fire engine.

Bert nearly jumped out of his armour. Lantern flattened his ears and lifted his tail to poop.

"That bird knows exactly how to set my nerves on edge," said the knight.

Sausage wouldn't sound an alarm unless she was worried.

I checked behind us. There was no sinister figure all in black. But there was a dragon eating a park bench.

Firepuffles swallowed the last of it, stretched

her neck forward and belched, setting a row of trees on fire. She flicked her tail and knocked a statue of a man on a horse off its plinth. Bert, of course, remained oblivious.

Scrambling on to a bench, I threw myself on Lantern.

"Move it, Bert!" I hissed.

"I'm afraid don't have a single ounce of energy left in me, Ollo."

"Do you want to fight a dragon?"

"Heavens, no!" he snorted. "They're far too dangerous in this sad and desolate place."

"In that case you might want to step on it, because Firepuffles is here," I said.

"What?" said the knight.

I sighed and grabbed the reins. There was no way Lantern could outrun the dragon, so I steered him behind a long, high hedge, hoping that Firepuffles hadn't seen us.

Sausage fluttered down on to my shoulder, her head swivelling in every direction.

The ground shook as Firepuffles landed on the other side of the hedge from us. We listened as the dragon sniffed the air, a snarl catching at the back of her throat.

I put my hand on Bert's shoulder to stop his armour from clanging.

We kept very, very still.

And then, Lantern sneezed.

I held my breath.

The dragon's head exploded through the hedge, sending twigs and leaves everywhere.

Lantern took fright, reared and set off at a trot.

"Is there any way he can go faster?" I shouted.

"Sugar lumps should do it," Bert spluttered.

I reached into my bag and brought out the strawberry laces the Dream HQ had given me. Ripping them into smaller pieces, I passed them to Bert.

"Try these!" I said.

The knight leaned forward and gave them to Lantern. He munched a handful, and then carried on at exactly the same speed.

Firepuffles tore through the hedge, flattening it. She snapped her head in our direction, plumes of smoke flooding from her nostrils.

Just as I was sure we were done for, Lantern kicked his front legs out and bolted through a gap in the hedge. Bert and I were so surprised we nearly fell off. Lantern galloped into the skate park and shot straight up the quarter pipe ramp, sailing over the edge of it and landing hard on the concrete. Lantern snorted and flicked his tail, orange sparks trailing from his hooves as he thundered towards the park gates.

Firepuffles spread her huge wings and took off, whipping the tops of the trees into a frenzy. Her shadow blotted out the sun, casting us into darkness.

"Ollo! Do something!" cried out the knight. "I want to go home to Eldermere Forest; I don't want to end up in the spirit world."

If only I had listened, I thought, *to Mr Curley and Seraphina.* And then I realized. Seraphina. She might be able to help.

But first we'd need to lose the dragon.

"Sausage!" I yelled. "Follow us!" If we could reach the underpass, we would be safe, as the tunnels were too narrow for Firepuffles to fit inside.

We stormed out of the park, turning sharp right,

clearing a low hedge and a car park barrier in quick succession.

A jet of flames hit the bin next to us, which erupted into a ball of fire. I cracked the reins and cut a path through a flower display towards the underpass. Lantern tore down the concrete slope and skidded around the corner, his hooves clattering, as we entered the tunnel. The horse drew to a halt halfway down the passageway, his mane damp as he shook his head.

"Where's Sausage?" I said.

"Can I open my eyes now?" asked Bert.

The ground beneath us began to vibrate, and cracks snaked their way along the walls and ceiling of the tunnel. Dust showered down around us, making Bert cough. The dim lights in the tunnel trembled as if they too were frightened.

The dragon's head filled the opening to the underpass, her red eyes gleaming like car tail lights. Firepuffles's scales flashed viper green as she lowered her head and sniffed the air. A noise rumbled deep in her throat. The dragon crouched and opened her jaws. I'd no idea so many teeth could fit into the one mouth. She took a breath.

If Firepuffles fired a jet of flames we'd be cooked alive in the tunnel!

All of a sudden, Sausage spiralled past the dragon, honking like a car horn. Firepuffles straightened up and lashed out at the bird with her claws. The bird, tiny next to the dragon, nipped nimbly out of her way.

I grasped Lantern's reins and squeezed his sides with my legs. The horse took off as the dragon screeched. A yellow light bathed the tunnel and a searing heat hit us. Just as I was sure we'd be engulfed by the flames, Lantern veered left and escaped into the darkness of an adjoining passageway.

We slowed to a halt. I leapt off the horse, checking his legs and tail for injuries, but he was fine.

"Are you OK, Bert?" I asked.

The knight took off his helmet and hid his face behind his shield.

"I thought I was going to be roasted like a suckling pig at a banquet." His shoulders heaved up and down.

I rifled around in my rucksack then handed

him a crumpled paper sweetie bag. Lantern's eyes widened as the sound of Bert blowing his nose echoed around the passageway.

I couldn't see Sausage. Pulling out my sword, I jogged back towards the main tunnel.

Flattening myself against the wall, I edged along it until I reached the end, where my foot hit something.

"*Knickers,*" croaked a small voice in the dark.

I put my sword away, crouched down and scooped Sausage up. Her tail feathers had been singed and there was a scorch mark on her back. She'd been caught by the dragon's fire. "Thanks for what you did, Sausage. Don't worry, Seraphina is the very person to fix you up. "

I hurried back to Lantern and Bert and placed Sausage in the knight's saddlebag.

"Bert, you ready?"

The knight sniffed and dabbed his eyes with the sweetie bag. "Almost," he said.

We set off through the tunnels, searching for a dragon-free exit. As we finally emerged into the daylight, I couldn't shake the thought that we were running out of time to stop Myrdina.

If it hadn't already run out.

I inched forward, looking left, right and then up above for the dragon. When I was sure it was clear, I peered through the window of Little Whispers Café. Candles flickered on the tables, making it warm and inviting as the light outside started to fade. Framed pictures of unicorns, wizards and faeries hung on the walls. But Seraphina was nowhere to be seen.

Bert tethered Lantern to a drainpipe and I went inside, with Sausage under my arm. The knight threw himself inside after me, relieved to be indoors.

I was about to call out for Seraphina when Bert tapped me on the shoulder and jabbed his finger towards a serving hatch in the wall.

The doors were ajar and a swirl of mist escaped through the gap.

I reached to my belt and brought the wooden sword out.

The knight clung to my arm.

I tightened my grip on Sausage and crept over to the hatch. I took a deep breath and, bracing myself for the worst, pulled the doors wide open.

A face loomed out of the mist and I yelled, dropping my sword.

Seraphina coughed as she waved a dish towel around, trying to clear the air. "Sorry, it's a bit smoky in here, isn't it? I thought if I had some toast it'd stop me from eating the red velvet cake but I've gone and burned it." The medium paused, her earrings swinging as she leaned through the window. "What have you got here?"

"This is Sausage and she's injured." I decided not to mention the bird had been hurt by a fire-breathing dragon.

Seraphina came flying out of the kitchen, wiping her hands on her apron. She took the bird from me.

"Who's the boy in the fancy dress?" she asked.

"He's an ex-knight called Bert," I said. "Bert, this is Seraphina. She's a spirit medium and healer."

Seraphina carried Sausage over to the sink, where she turned the tap on. Sausage flapped her wings until she became used to the flow of cool water and settled, soothed by it.

"This is one lucky soul," said Seraphina,

examining Sausage. "She'll be as right as rain once I pop a bandage on her." She rummaged around under the sink for a first aid box. As she bandaged Sausage's wound, she paused, as though someone had interrupted her, waited a moment and then set the bird on the counter. Seraphina gave Sausage a piece of fresh roll to peck at. The medium's eyebrows rose in surprise as the bird thanked her, happy to be fed.

Finally, Seraphina took off her apron. Her T-shirt had the words *Frankie Says Relax* on it and right now I wished that Seraphina would take Frankie's advice, whoever he was.

"What have you done, Ollo?"

"I don't know what you mean."

"My spirit guides tell me you gave in to temptation! After all their warnings!"

I lowered my gaze and rubbed the sides of my shoes together so they squeaked. I could feel my face turning a deeper shade of red than Seraphina's nail varnish. "If I could go back and undo everything that's happened, I would in a heartbeat. And if you don't believe me, ask your spirit guides. They know it's the truth."

Bert laid his shield down on a table. "There is an extensive list of catastrophic events that have happened because Ollo couldn't resist having a dream – me being here, to start with."

"Thanks for that, Bert," I sniffed.

"However, things are going to be a lot worse if Ollo doesn't catch a lady called Myrdina, who is the Mother of All Nightmares. She is running around the town petrifying children so she has the energy to finally leave her world for this one. Ollo wants to use some dream essence to imprison Myrdina. But the Mother of All Nightmares is always one step ahead of us. Perhaps you know her whereabouts so that we might be able to thwart her, once and for all."

Seraphina stood staring at us with her mouth open, not saying a word.

Bert glanced over to me, his brows knitted together, not sure what to do next. "Do you have to be dead for this medium to hear you?"

"I know it's a lot to take in, Seraphina, but it's all true. We wouldn't ask for your help unless we really needed it." I touched her on the arm. "Are you OK?"

"I'm fine – at least I think I am. It's just I could have sworn I saw a dragon on the street."

"That's Firepuffles – Ollo released her too. If you'll both excuse me." Bert dropped to the floor and crawled under a table for cover.

"By accident," I added. "I did all those things by accident."

Seraphina looked at me. "I'm not going to give you a lecture, Ollo, because you've got cloth ears and won't take a blind bit of notice. However, it seems to me there is a chance you can put some of this right, and if there is, then I will do my best to help you. We better get cracking."

Seraphina went to the back of the shop and fetched a black velvet bag. Opening it, she brought out a copy of *Psychic Times*, a corkscrew and a packet of crisps, before retrieving a thick bundle of dried herbs. She lit them, blew out the flames and wafted the herbs around the place, making Bert sneeze.

"I'm cleansing the space of negative energy," she said.

Sausage hopped over to the edge of the counter, curious as to what was going on.

The medium brought out a dark green knitted shawl, which she shook out and placed around her shoulders.

"Does the garment have ancient mystical powers that allow you to connect with your ancestors?" said Bert.

"No, I'm chilly," replied Seraphina. "My spirit guides will be able to find her quicker if you have something that belongs to the Mother of All Nightmares?"

"Bert? Sausage? Anything?" I asked.

Bert shook his head and Sausage blew a raspberry.

"In that case I'll need to hold your hands, Ollo," said Seraphina. "If I can see clearly into your mind, I'll get a look at Myrdina and my guides should be able to pick up some clues."

I placed my rucksack on the ground, took off my coat, pulled the chair up to the table and sat. Seraphina took my hands in hers. My fingers tingled.

"If you could picture the Mother of All Nightmares for me," she said.

I closed my eyes and thought back to Myrdina standing in the doorway of the cottage. Her flower-patterned lace veil rippled in the wind. There were dark hollows where her eyes should be and red lipstick was smudged around her mouth. Her black dress rustled and gleamed in the sunlight, and the masks stared, their mouths widening as they grinned. Mist floated over the flagstones, hiding the ivy and chilling the air.

The terror of her being so close rose up in my throat.

My eyes shot open as the medium's hand fluttered up to her heart. She took a while to steady her breath. "I'm sorry. That image you showed me of her was vivid and her energy was so evil, I had to disconnect. This woman is dangerous, Ollo."

"That's why we need to find her as soon as possible," I said.

Seraphina hesitated. "Do you wish me to proceed?"

"She does," said Bert from the floor.

"I do." I gave her a firm nod.

"Let me see if my spirit guides can locate her." The medium placed her hands on the table and spread her fingers out. She dipped her head down; the roots of her hair were as white as snowy owls.

Sausage sat blinking, nestled in between some table mats and blue napkins.

"Myrdina is close," announced Seraphina.

Bert's armour rattled and I raised my finger to my lips, afraid he'd interrupt Seraphina's concentration.

The medium's eyelids fluttered. "My guides are showing her to me: she's surrounded by clouds and a veil is whipping around her head. I can hear whispering, but her mouth is not moving. There's a black book – she's holding it open and I believe what looks like shadows are tumbling from it."

I leapt to my feet.

"The Book of Nightmares!" Floorboards grumbled as I paced up and down. "I'm not sure what she's up to, but whatever it is, it won't be good."

Sausage whistled in agreement.

"Where is she?" said Bert in a voice that was barely a whisper.

"If she's surrounded by clouds then she's high up – but there are no mountains here." All of a sudden it came to me. "The roof of the high-rise!"

"But why would she go there?" asked the knight.

"Because there are a whole load of kids in the one place she can scare. And that'll make it easier for her to collect the last of the energy she needs." I threw on my coat, grabbing my sword and rucksack. "Thank you for your help, Seraphina. We need to go! Now!"

Seraphina stood. "Ollo, the spirits have one more message for you, and this time you must listen." I stopped. *"Stay away from the water – and if you are in over your head . . . the only way is up."*

I frowned, not sure what the spirits meant.

"I promise I'll keep away from the water." I reached under the table for Bert and dragged him out from underneath it. I hauled him to his feet and pushed him towards the door.

Sausage glided over the tables to land on my shoulder.

"Ollo!" said Seraphina. "Be careful! This nightmare does not walk alone."

I stepped out into the dusk, the medium's words ringing in my ears.

CHAPTER 15

The pink-and-gold-tinged clouds darkened to more sombre blues, greys and purples as we sped towards the high-rise that loomed up from the town like a giant ghostly domino. Even though it was June, there was an iciness in the air.

Lantern had slowed again and I'd run out of strawberry laces. We trotted through the underpass and emerged on to the street, which was deserted. As we travelled under some trees, I noticed skeleton-white leaves falling from their branches. Clusters of mushrooms sprouted from kerbsides, flowers had wilted, and clumps of broken spiderwebs hung down from telephone wires like dirty washing.

Myrdina must be gaining in strength for this to be happening.

I slid off Lantern as we arrived outside the flats and squinted upwards at the roof. It made me feel dizzy. I was so busy imagining the awful things Myrdina might be up to that I didn't notice Bert doing a runner until he was halfway down the road.

I chased after him, yelling. When I caught up with the knight, I wheeled him around with so much force, something flew out from his tunic pocket and bounced on the ground twice before it settled. I picked up a small orange bottle labelled *Balloon Bubbles*.

"Did you steal this from Dream HQ?"

"You're not exactly in a position to tell me off about pinching things." He shrugged. "You don't get balloons in A Knight's Adventure and I wanted to take some home."

"You and those balloons won't be going anywhere unless you step up." I threw the bottle into my rucksack.

Bert raised his voice. "The Mother of All Nightmares is on that roof. She's turning all the children to stone, and I don't want that happening to me. You're the one who released that monster; you can deal with her. I'm done here!" Bert walked into the nearest bush and sat down.

The heavens opened and the rain fell at a slant from the sky like grey needles. We were wasting valuable time. I pulled my hood up and crouched in front of the shrubs, which were a sickly yellow colour.

"*Bertrand Ponce de Leon!* You took an oath, remember? You're not an ordinary boy, you're a knight."

"*Leave me alone!*"

"Think about all those children inside that tower block. You're not risking your life for me. You're doing it for them." I wiped the rain from my face and softened my voice. "Bert, everyone gets scared and that's OK. It just means you're about to do something really brave."

I could hear the rain striking his armour.

"What if you don't manage to capture her?" he asked.

"Then I'll face the consequences. It's better to try than to walk away. And besides, what can go wrong with you, me, Sausage and Lantern working together as a team?" I flashed a smile at him, not sure if he could see it or not.

The bush quivered as he appeared. He stared at me for a moment. "I was only pretending to be the hero in A Knight's Adventure. I was just acting brave – I've never actually had to be brave."

"Well, now's the perfect opportunity to show everyone what you're really capable of. But we'll need to get a move on."

Sausage dive-bombed us, ticking loudly. Time was running out.

"Fine. I will assist on two conditions," he said. "The first is that Lantern is kept safe, out here, and the second is that upon capture of Myrdina, you'll make it your immediate priority to ensure the horse, the dragon and I have safe passage to Eldermere Forest."

"It's a deal!" I said, sticking my hand out to shake his. Then I hauled him out of the bush.

Sausage zoomed towards the tower block and we

ran after her.

We raced up the steps, then I opened the door to the foyer and peered inside.

A thin mist flowed down the stairs and black mould crept across the paint-blistered walls.

There were strange shrieks and yells echoing around the place that made my blood run cold. My nerves snapped, crackled and popped more than a bowl of Rice Krispies.

"Bert, Sausage – here's the plan. We'll take the lift to the top floor and from there the stairs directly to the roof."

"Then what?" asked Bert.

"We need to lure her over to me, so I can give her a drop of the dream essence," I said. "What's the one thing she can't resist?"

"Being frightful," said Bert.

"Apart from that."

"Well, that's obvious. She can't resist scaring children."

"That's it! Perhaps we can fool her into thinking there's a child on the roof. That would bring her over to us in an instant."

Sausage opened her beak and made the same noise as a wailing toddler, startling the knight and me.

I grinned at her. "You're a genius, Sausage. That should do the trick."

"And I could distract her with some nifty sword work while you give her the potion," said the knight, beaming.

"Good idea, Bert," I said. "Let's go!"

Sausage slipped in through the door and circled the foyer. Satisfied it was clear, she swooped around trumpeting.

Bert looked as though he was willing himself to be brave as he drew his sword.

I ducked inside and dashed across to the lifts, pressing both buttons. The cables twanged as they raced each other towards the ground floor. Even though they were travelling at speed, I wished they would hurry up.

I gave Bert the thumbs up and beckoned him in to join us. He took a few steps forward and halted.

"Come on! What is there to worry about?" I said.

The air in the foyer cooled and a thin milky mist rippled in across the floor. Dirty cobwebs gathered and billowed like unwashed curtains over the windows.

The lights hummed, fizzled and dimmed.

A sudden movement caught my eye.

I blinked hard and there it was again.

An enormous shadow rose up behind Bert. It reached all the way up to the ceiling with a crooked body, long legs, and hands with clawlike fingers.

Bert lowered his sword and shield. "Ollo, why are you gawping at me like I've got two heads?"

My throat tightened.

"There's something behind me, isn't there?" said Bert.

The shadow's bony fingers reached out for the knight.

I found my voice. *"RUN, Bert!"*

The lift doors pinged and I flung myself inside, jamming them open. The knight charged at lightning speed and sprang forward. As he landed next to me, the shadow shot over the floor and lunged, grabbing hold of his leg. Bert wobbled, lost his balance and fell.

"Do something!" he pleaded as he was dragged away, his fingernails raking the floor.

I chased after the shadow, swiping my sword at it, just as Bert had taught me. The wooden blade sailed through the creature as though it was made of air.

Sausage let rip with the roar of a lion, flew at the shadow with her talons out and passed straight through it. She fluttered over to the doors, where she crash-landed on the ground.

The shadow lifted the knight up by his ankles, dangling him upside down. Bert's shield fell, striking the floor.

I stared up at the monstrous dark shape. I could just make out two white holes where its eyes were, and I gulped.

It only seemed to be made of shadow and nothing else. When I got scared of shadows in my room at night, I'd switch my lamp on and they'd always disappear.

I reached into my rucksack, my hand scrabbling around until I found the torch Dream HQ had given me. Flicking it on, I shone it directly at the shadow's bony arm. The shadow hissed as its arm disappeared and Bert dropped to the floor. I gripped on to the torch with both hands and remembered being blinded by the sunlight in Eldermere Forest. I shone the beam of light directly at the shadow's head, so it couldn't see where Bert was. It gurgled and retreated. The knight snatched up his shield, scurrying forward on his hands and knees until he'd made it to the lift, where he scooted into the corner.

I backed across the foyer, careful to keep the torch pointed at the shadow.

"Sausage! Hurry!" I cried out. I stumbled and dropped the torch, watching in horror as it rolled away from me. The shadow sprang up and hurtled towards us faster than a shark about to attack. I whacked the buttons on the panel and the doors began to close. Just as they were about to bang shut, Sausage squeezed in through the narrow gap, squawking.

The shadow pounded on the metal and it began to buckle.

I held my breath until we started to lurch upwards towards the seventeenth floor. I slid down the wall, collapsing in a heap beside Bert.

"Next time you tell me there's *nothing to worry about*, I'll know my life is in terrible danger," said the knight, furious. "What on earth was that thing anyway? It stung every time it touched me. That was a complete *nightmare*."

The lift creaked as it pulled us ever closer to the roof.

"A nightmare. Oh no, Bert. That's it!" I buried my face in my hands.

"*What?*" said the knight, agitated.

Sausage hopped on Bert's shoulder, gazing at me.

"That's *exactly* what that shadow monster was – *a nightmare*. Seraphina told us her spirit guides saw Myrdina with the Book of Nightmares. It must have been the masks that were whispering. She's bringing all the children's bad dreams to life!"

"*Scary biscuits,*" said Sausage out of nowhere.

"Think about it. How else is she going to make sure she can frighten enough children to bring her here for good? If she releases a whole book of nightmares, she'll be able to petrify every single child in the town and quite possibly beyond."

"*Knickers,*" said Sausage.

"Couldn't have put it better myself," said Bert. "Have I got this right? Are you saying there are actually real live nightmares roaming around this building?"

"It would explain what that thing was that attacked us in the foyer." If it wasn't awful enough having to face Myrdina, we now had the possibility of bumping into nightmares along the way. Seraphina had warned as much. She had said Myrdina *does not walk alone*.

I closed my eyes for a second and rested my head on my knees. I longed to go home and put the telly on. I missed squabbling with Kyle over the TV remote and playing best of three paper, scissors, stone to see who could get out of doing the dishes. I hoped that Mum and Dad were OK, and prayed that if I could trap Myrdina, her magic would be undone and they'd be themselves again.

The lift groaned as it slowed. I glanced up to see we were stopping at the sixteenth floor, not the seventeenth.

I got to my feet. Bert stood with his shield at the ready and shuffled behind me. Sausage shook out her wings in readiness.

I braced myself as the doors opened.

No one was there.

I stuck my head out.

"Can you see anything?" whispered the knight.

The place smelled strange: exactly the same as the seaside but without the fresh breeze or whiff of vinegary chips. Fronds of dark green seaweed glistened from the red fire extinguishers. Sausage chased after a brown crab that scuttled sideways across the floor. A starfish was stuck to the wall and a scattering of pastel-coloured broken shells were dotted around the length of the passageway. The fire doors had been ripped off their hinges and lay on the ground with their glass missing.

Something very odd had happened here.

I noticed a girl further up the corridor.

"Hello?" I called.

There was no reply.

"What are you doing? You don't know what's out there," hissed Bert.

"I think someone might need our help," I answered, and stepped out of the lift.

The crab swiped its claw at Sausage, making her screech. She flapped up to settle on my shoulder and clicked her beak nervously in my ear. Bert, not wanting to be left on his own, followed us, muttering under his breath.

The doors closed behind him and the lift whirred into action before disappearing off to one of the floors below.

"Oh, that's just marvellous! Now there's no way out of here!" said the knight.

I saw a giant puddle on the floor. *Stay away from water*, Seraphina had said. I walked carefully around it.

The girl had her back to me. I hesitated, watching her like a hawk, the shadowy nightmare from the foyer fresh on my mind. Carefully, I drew closer, until I could see her face.

It was Jeannie!

She must have come to the flats looking for me with Roxy Patterson.

Her face was fixed in an expression I'd never seen before – like an actor in one of the scary films I'm not supposed to watch on Netflix. Jeannie's arms were raised, as if she was trying to protect herself from something. I reached out to touch her; her skin was cold as the pavement. She was a darker grey than any of the others I'd seen, as though she'd been in out in the rain.

I couldn't imagine what had terrified her so much, but there was a good chance it might still be here.

Sausage gave a long, low whistle.

Bert stayed well back. "Can we go now?" he said.

There wasn't much I could do for Jeannie. Once I might have wanted this – revenge for choosing Roxy Patterson over me. But now, I hated that this had happened to her. I could see every single line of fear etched on her face, and nobody deserved to be that frightened.

Sausage gave a sharp blast, like a fog horn.

I raised my head; a roaring noise filling my ears.

At the end of the corridor, an enormous wave reared up. It gathered pace as it rolled along the landing towards us, its crest as white as brand-new trainers.

No wonder Jeannie had been so petrified. She'd

always been afraid of the water because she couldn't swim.

We turned and ran.

"There are stairs halfway down the landing, it's our only way out," I said.

The wave knocked out the lights as it exploded through the door.

Sausage flashed down the passageway, searching for the stairs. She hovered by the exit sign as the knight and I sprinted forward, dodging an assault course of broken wood, rocks and jellyfish.

All of a sudden, my foot caught on some blue rope and I went flying, sprawling on the floor. I scrambled upright and kept running.

Bert stood in the doorway, waiting to grab me to safety, but I was too slow.

I saw by the look on his face what was coming.

The wall of water crashed over me, the weight of it knocking me off my feet and sweeping me forward. Its iciness hit me like an avalanche. I was spun round and round, my clothes being tugged in different directions, no longer sure if I was the right way up. All around me a shoal of white bubbles fizzled. I peered into the gloom, blinking, sure I could see dark shapes cutting through the murk.

My lungs began to burn.

I thought about Mr Curley and the Dream Store. I wished I was back there, making DreamDrops with him and Sausage.

Seraphina's voice warning me about the water swam around inside my head. *The only way is up*, the spirits had said.

In a flash it came back to me that I'd put the bottle of Balloon Bubbles in my bag. Bubbles would float upwards, wouldn't they? I'd be able to work out which way it was to the surface.

I stuck my hand in my bag and searched for the small glass container. After what seemed like ages, my cold fingers found the bottle and brought it out. Careful not to let go of it, I unscrewed the lid and shook it, releasing some of the bubbles. There were some dull pops and a rainbow of balloons appeared that shot down below me, their strings trailing after them.

I must be upside down!

Using my arms to spin myself around, I kicked

with all my might, but the current was relentless. My throat closed. I released the rest of the Balloon Bubbles into the water. As they inflated in reds, yellows, blues, whites and pinks, I grasped on to their strings with both hands and held on tight. They pulled me upwards. Just as my vision began to blur, I burst through the surface of the water. My mouth opened wide as I gasped for air, gulping it down, while I flayed my arms and kicked my legs to stay afloat. The wave whisked me along the corridor.

That's when I saw the water was pouring out of four large smashed windows at the end of the passageway. If I didn't do something fast, I was going to be emptied out from the sixteenth floor on to the concrete below.

I gave up trying to swim against the current and looked around for something to grab hold of, but everything was passing by too fast.

Sailing through the last of the fire doors, I spotted a red exit sign hanging down from the ceiling. I steered myself into the middle of the water and raised my hands, wincing as I slammed into the sign. I clung on to it like a limpet to a rock, certain my arms would be wrenched from their sockets. Gritting my teeth, I closed my eyes and held on. Gradually, I began to feel the pull of the water lessen as it poured out from the windows, but the weight of my body grew so heavy – I couldn't help it; I let go. I landed with a splash, and then my feet hit something solid. I opened my eyes to discover the bulk of the water had drained away and I was in the shallows.

"Ollo!" said Bert.

Sausage zigzagged towards me, cheering and whistling. She flew on to my shoulder and pulled some seaweed from my ear.

"When that wave hit you, I thought you were done for. Which was *awful* because Lantern and I'd be stuck here for ever," said the knight.

"Nice to see you too, Bert," I rasped.

A rumble sounded along the corridor. Another wave had risen, even bigger than the last one, and was barrelling towards us.

Bert hauled me up, putting my arm over his shoulder. I limped along the passageway until we'd made it safely into the stairwell. The wave thundered past, sending a jet of spray under the gap in the door.

We'd escaped with our lives, but I couldn't help feeling there was much worse to come.

My breath was laboured and my wet clothes uncomfortable, but there was no time to rest. Sausage flitted as silent as a bat up ahead as Bert and I began to climb the stairs towards the Mother of All Nightmares.

CHAPTER 16

A thick mist cascaded down the steps and the lights on the walls flickered as if there were moths trapped inside them. The handrail was furred with clumps of cobwebs that blew in the breeze like grey windsocks.

Somewhere in the stairwell, a door was banging, setting my nerves on edge.

I knew from the times my friends and I had explored the high-rise that the exit to the roof was always locked. As we neared the top of the stairs, I could see the door had been wrenched from its hinges and the security camera smashed.

"Bert!" I said, stopping to catch my breath. "Myrdina feeds off fear. So no matter what happens, don't show her any."

"Me? Frightened? Never!" said the knight, glancing nervously at the door.

"We'll need to keep out of sight so Myrdina doesn't spot us. Sausage, would you mind going into my pocket?" I held it open for her and she swooped into it. "And we have to be quiet."

Bert dropped his sword, the noise of it echoing around the staircase. "Um, sorry!"

He took hold of my arm. "Let me go first, Ollo. You're right: I swore an oath and I'm just as much of a knight here as I am back home."

"That's more like the legend I remember from Camp de Leon," I said.

Steel ground against steel as he brought his sword out and raised his shield. The knight strode forward with his head held high.

Taking a deep breath, I followed him outside. Bert flattened himself against a wall and peered around it.

Clouds had blindfolded the moon and kidnapped

the stars. Dark puddles shivered all over the roof. The wind whipped against the building. I staggered to the edge of the roof, gripping on to railings so cold, they drained the warmth from my body. Two horizontal metal bars were all that stood between me and a never-ending drop. I glanced down, my stomach somersaulting. Orange and yellow lights winked below as if the heavens had been tipped upside down.

I backed away, feeling sick. On the far side of the building, I could see the pine trees poking through the hole the dragon had made in my ceiling.

The wind died away suddenly and everything stilled. A bank of dense fog rolled in. In seconds, I'd lost sight of the knight. I'd no idea how close I was to the edge of the high-rise. Sausage wriggled around inside my pocket.

I stood still, shivering in my damp clothes, listening out for Bert. I wished the knight was where he usually was: right behind me. "OK, Sausage," I whispered. "Let's see if we can bring Myrdina to us."

The mynah bird zoomed into the air, wailing like a child in distress. The fog began to curl around my legs. Drawing my sword, I hacked at the tendrils, freeing myself. I swiped the weapon all around me to keep the mist away.

Spotting a figure in the milky gloom up ahead, I darted forward, my feet splashing through the puddles.

"Bert?"

The mist dissolved and the Mother of All Nightmares lunged towards me, grasping hold of my wrist. "Think you can trick me, do you? I could smell you from a mile off, Ollo," she said. "Oh, the fun I'm going to have with you." Her sunken eyes burned through her veil and her lipstick had bled down to her chin.

Horrified, I shook myself free and stumbled. That's when I saw her skirt glowing a sickly green that lit up the fringes of the fog.

Only one of the masks remained black.

They began to whisper and white worms of fungus sprouted out from my sword. It crumbled to sawdust in front of my eyes and scattered over the rooftop.

I grabbed the dream essence and began to

unscrew the lid. I had to end this before the last mask was illuminated. The concentrate was strong: if I'd mixed it correctly, one small drop should be all I needed to imprison her.

I sprung towards Myrdina, raising the bottle.

She vanished in a puff of screams and reappeared behind me. In one swift move, she seized the dream essence, yanking it out of my fingers.

"*No!*" I yelled.

Myrdina pressed the bottle against the mask in the middle of her skirts. Its mouth stretched open and snapped shut, sealing the dream essence in behind it.

My eyes stung.

Myrdina stroked the face of the remaining black mask on her skirts. "I've saved this one until last. I want it to be your fear that lights it up," she said.

A shiver travelled along every bone in my spine.

She circled around me. "What scares you, Ollo? What curdles your blood? What causes your heart to hammer so fast, you're worried it'll break?" She watched me with interest. "Would it be this?"

The masks muttered and the wind moved some

of the fog away on the other side of the roof. I saw Firepuffles land, flapping her gigantic wings. And I saw Bert, backing away, letting his sword and shield fall to the ground. Myrdina chuckled.

As a jet of flames shot out from the dragon's mouth, Bert screamed and the fog rolled back in, blocking my view.

I'd already lost my friends because of Roxy Patterson. I couldn't bear to lose another.

My cries echoed around the rooftop and my fear changed the last mask from black to a putrid green colour. I wiped the tears from my face.

Bert was gone. I couldn't let the Mother of All Nightmares win, otherwise Bert's life would have been lost for nothing.

I was determined not to show her any fear.

I closed my eyes for a second and cleared my mind of all thoughts.

The mask on her skirts flickered and returned to black.

Myrdina glided towards me and I backed away from her. "Everyone has their limits, Ollo. What makes you sick to your stomach?" She leaned closer.

"Perhaps it is this?"

The fog thinned and disappeared, revealing bent and twisted railings on either side of me. I teetered on the ledge of the building. Behind was nothing but the wind, rain and inky darkness. I held on to what was left of the barrier, my insides heaving.

"Are you feeling a bit on edge?" asked Myrdina.

The mouths on the masks creaked as they stretched into grins.

The wind cut through me like a knife. I willed myself to keep my mind blank. I held on to the bars so tight, I couldn't feel my fingers.

"Look at me, Ollo. I want to see the fear that's going to let me scare children all day, every day." Myrdina bent the fingers back on my hand and I let go of the railing.

I swayed as she knocked my other hand away.

"It's no use fighting it." Myrdina smoothed her veil and skirts down. The mist behind her darkened and shifted. "The knight attempted to be brave too – and it didn't exactly end well for him."

It came flooding back to me. The horror of what

the dragon had done to Bert.

"That's it, Ollo. Let it all out," cooed the Mother of All Nightmares.

The last mask began to flicker green.

All of a sudden, a voice shouted out, *"Potius ingenio quam vi."*

I sucked my breath in. I'd heard those same words before, deep in Eldermere Forest.

The knight emerged from the fog, his sword flashing silver. Firepuffles stood beside him.

He was alive!

Firepuffles hadn't harmed him!

The knight charged at the Mother of All Nightmares, who stood her ground as the masks began to hiss and mutter. The mist grew in height and sped towards the knight and Firepuffles in thick tendrils that wound themselves round and round Bert's sword and the dragon's muzzle. It engulfed them until they could no longer move. No matter how much the knight and the dragon fought, they were stuck like spider-wrapped flies in webs.

Myrdina watched as they were dragged towards

the edge of the roof and dangled over the side of it.

Out from nowhere, there was the sound of a low whistle like a bomb dropping from a great height, and a bird swooped in, flying straight into Myrdina's veil. The Mother of All Nightmares took a swipe at Sausage, hitting her. The bird crashed to the ground and lay still.

Myrdina advanced towards Sausage, and my insides burned red hot.

I saw my chance.

I let go of the railings and hurled myself at the Mother of All Nightmares. Crouching down, I plunged my hand into the mouth of the mask that contained the dream essence. Teeth scraped my knuckles as I pushed as far back as I could, desperate to find the bottle.

If the masks were giving Myrdina her power, they would also pass on the dream essence.

Sifting through warm slime, my fingers finally curled around the neck of the bottle and popped the lid off. I tipped the bottle on its side to release the liquid. I yanked my hand back out, shaking green gunk from my fingers.

Myrdina turned on me. "I've had enough of you,

Ollo. It's time for me to enter this world and for you to leave it." A tendril of fog slammed into me and I flew through the gap in the railings, off the side of the building. My hands raked the air, and at the very last second, I latched on to the rough concrete ledge. Kicking my legs, I concentrated hard on looking up as my body swung in the wind.

The Mother of All Nightmares lifted a foot and brought it down on to my fingers, the grit on the sole of her boot pressing into my skin. Lightning smashed the black sky overhead and the puddles flashed as I cried out in pain.

Bert heard me and struggled within his mist prison. Firepuffles snorted, but she was stuck fast too.

Every single mask was still green.

The dream essence hadn't worked; I must have got the mix wrong.

"You released me, Ollo; now it's my turn to release you," she crowed, pressing down on my fingers with the heel of her boot.

A dark cloud floated towards the roof. It flickered and boomed, making the puddles jump. I watched as it headed directly into the wind. Lightning scratched the sky and struck the top of the roof.

My eyes widened and I forgot about the searing pain in my hand. The cloud was coming straight for us and much bigger than I had imagined it would be. I could feel everything being tugged up towards it as if it was magnetic.

Myrdina stiffened.

The masks on her skirts began to blink. One by one, their green lights fizzled out. Myrdina screamed and dropped to her knees, every last one of the masks turning back to black.

The cloud hovered directly over Myrdina.

"What have you done?" she whispered, her head tilting upwards. There was a crack of thunder and the underside of the cloud opened up. A light shone from its centre, dazzling us for a second. Then I saw the rows of long jagged teeth part, ready to swallow Myrdina whole.

"Make it stop! Don't do this, Ollo," she croaked frantically. "I'll give you all the gold coins you could ever wish for. Don't trap me in the dream world again. I couldn't stand it. I promise I won't turn any more children into stone." The masks began to whisper. Lightning forked down all around her, silencing them.

"This isn't over. I'll come for you, Ollo, and that's a promise," growled Myrdina.

The cloud dipped down and covered her head, silencing her, much to my relief. As her skirts and the masks and her boots disappeared from view, the air filled with the screams of children. The teeth in the cloud snapped shut, sealing the Mother of All Nightmares inside. The cloud lifted, glowing red as it drifted silently past the moon on its way to the dream world.

The mist began to dissolve, releasing Bert, who plummeted off the side of the building. Firepuffles shook the last of the fog off her and dived down to catch the knight on her back. In a beat of wings, she carried Bert to the roof, where he fell off her and crumpled on the ground.

I tried to pull myself up, but I was too weak. I wasn't sure how much longer I'd be able to hold on.

Sausage hopped on to the ledge and peered down at me. "*Knickers,*" said the bird before taking off, blaring like an ambulance.

It wasn't long before I heard a familiar clanking sound and Bert appeared just in the nick of time. Taking hold of my arms, he grunted as he hauled me back up to safety. I sat, stunned, on the roof. Sausage landed on my shoulder and nuzzled into my neck, comforting me.

"Are you unharmed, Ollo?" asked Bert, whisking out his hip flask from his tunic. "You look like you could do with some mead."

I pushed it away and shrank back as Firepuffles thundered over to us, shooting jets of flame into the sky.

"I thought you were toast!" I wailed. "I saw her attack you."

The knight smiled. "It was a close call, Ollo. It was only when I sang our song that she finally remembered who I was and returned to her usual lovely self again, thank the gods."

"What was the song?"

"'Puff the Magic Dragon'," he said with a shrug as he patted Firepuffles, who bent to sniff the top of my head. She licked my face, covering it in a thick slime that dripped on to Sausage, who shook herself vigorously.

"Ollo?"

"Yes, Bert?"

"Was that cloud the thing you made in Dream HQ with all those ingredients?"

"It was."

"Remind me never to get on the wrong side of you," he said. "Now that Myrdina is trapped in the dream world, can Lantern, Firepuffles and I go home?"

"A promise is a promise," I said, on our way to the exit.

Everything felt different as I eased myself down the steps. The black mould and spiderwebs had disappeared and there was a lightness in the air, as if all threat of danger had gone.

As we rounded the corner to the next set of stairs, Sausage clanged like a bell being rung at a boxing fight.

I reached for my sword, before remembering I didn't have one any more.

"I know you're there, *Ollo*. You can't hide from

me for ever."

I halted in my tracks. Her voice was enough to make every inch of my skin crawl.

Roxy Patterson was the last person I wanted to see right now.

The knight drew his sword and stepped in front of me. A long throaty growl escaped from Firepuffles.

I stood for a second or two, deciding what I should do.

"Wait here, Bert," I said. As much as I wished the knight and Firepuffles would sort her out for me, this was something I had to do on my own because they wouldn't be around every time I crossed paths with Roxy Patterson.

I walked down the last of the steps and turned the corner.

When I saw her, I gripped on to the handrail to steady myself.

Roxy Patterson was leaning against the wall, one leg tucked behind her as if she was casually waiting for a bus. There were shadows under her eyes, but I couldn't tell if it was because it was late or because her eyeliner had smudged. Her fingers were covered in rings that were going to bruise my skin when she hit me.

"Did you really think I wouldn't find you?" she asked.

I opened my mouth but nothing came out. I licked my dry lips.

"This has been a long time coming," she said, pushing up the sleeves of her denim jacket. The gap where she'd lost her tooth gave her the appearance of a badly carved jack-o'-lantern.

I knew that glint in her eyes.

She came towards me and I shrank back, landing on the step behind me with a bump. Out of habit, I wrapped my arms over my head, waiting for the first blow.

And that's when it struck me: Roxy was no different from Myrdina. Both of them thrived on people's fear and I'd had enough. I lowered my arms and got to my feet.

"Did I say you could go?" asked Roxy, flexing her knuckles.

"You don't get to order me around any more,

Roxy Patterson," I said. "There's nothing wrong with me just because I'm different to you. I lied and stole to protect myself from you. I hated you for turning my friends against me. And worse than all of that, I hated myself for not standing up to you – until now. Don't come near me again."

Roxy opened her mouth, but I carried on.

"Just so we're clear: lay another finger on me and I'm going to tell the head teacher *everything*. You've been in serious trouble twice this term already, so you'll be expelled, and then you'll find out what it's like having no friends when you're trying to settle into your new school." I looked into her cold eyes and saw nothing but fear, loathing and misery lurking in their depths. There was no way Roxy would ever change her mind about me or feel sorry for what she'd done. With some people, all you can do is get your point across in a way you know they'll understand.

"One last thing. If you ever pick on me or anyone else at school again, my friends will pay you a visit, and that's a promise."

"Give me a break. You don't have any friends,"

she said, wrinkling her nose up.

Sausage flew past me at the speed of light and Roxy flattened herself against the wall. The knight appeared, drew both of his swords and twirled them around as he marched down the steps towards us and flanked my side.

Roxy's head swivelled in terror at Firepuffles's roar. She froze as the dragon sent a jet of flames in her direction. Roxy took off, screaming at the top of her lungs, and fled as fast as her legs would carry her.

"Big knickers in a twist," cackled Sausage as she opened her beak and nodded her head.

"Was that the school bully you needed help defending yourself against?" asked Bert, putting away his swords.

I sniffed as I nodded.

"You don't need a sword; words are your weapon. You're pretty fearsome. You could give Firepuffles a run for her money," he said.

A smile played on my lips as Bert, Sausage, Firepuffles and I walked through the doors into the corridor. We halted in our tracks, amazed to see all the smashed windows and debris from the giant tidal wave had vanished.

"Look! Jeannie's gone too!" I cried out. "Myrdina's magic must have been undone now that she's back in the dream world!" I spun around. "Mr Curley must be back to normal as well! He can help you home, Bert."

The knight frowned. "I don't know, Ollo. I watched the man trickle through your fingers."

"Come on, Bert! There's only one way to find out." The thought that Mr Curley was alive chased my aches and pains away.

Sausage did a loop the loop in the corridor, making the same noises as a marching band as she zoomed after us.

The wind rushed down Hidden Lane, pushing over bins and chasing empty chip wrappers over the cobblestones. The moon hid behind Firepuffles, who circled overhead. Bert steered Lantern straight for the patch of grass opposite the Dream Store.

The air cooled; a sign rain was on its way.

Bert and I dashed over to the shop. The window

was no longer cracked, the astronaut was flying around in her rocket and the planets shone bright as they hula-hooped their rings. The bell tinkled as we stepped inside, holding our breaths. Although it was dark, I could see the shattered glass had disappeared and the shelves once again gleamed with hundreds of bottles of DreamDrops.

I breathed in deep, smelling strawberries and cream, and I tingled with all the excitement and anticipation that had returned to the store.

Sausage sensed it as well and was too busy trumpeting to notice the figure that emerged from the emerald curtains.

"Oh, Mr Curley. *You are alive!*" I said.

The bird swooped to land on his shoulder and nibbled his ear. He patted her, frowning as he noticed the bandage around her middle.

Mr Curley cleared his throat and looked at me. "Ollo, there is no easy way for me to say this," he said quietly. "You stole a bottle of A Knight's Adventure from the Dream Factory and took a drop when I expressly asked you not to do so. The consequences of your actions have been highly damaging. I must ask you to leave . . . and never come back."

The rain hammered against the window. The lamp outside cast shadows of the drops running down Mr Curley's cheeks. For a second, I wished I had been turned to stone, so Mr Curley's words would not hurt so much.

My shoulders slumped. What he said was true. By taking the DreamDrops I had ruined everything.

There was something I had to do before I left.

"Mr Curley? This is Bertrand Ponce de Leon and he needs to return home to A Knight's Adventure with his horse and dragon."

Mr Curley said nothing.

"I brought them back against their will. None of them wished to be here, Mr Curley. It was all my fault."

He held his face still. It would have been more bearable if Mr Curley had shouted at me or at least thrown something to show how angry he was.

"I'll see to it they have safe passage back to A Knight's Adventure," he said. "Take the knight downstairs and say your goodbyes. You can leave through the courtyard."

"Mr Curley? I'm sorry for everything . . . and I'm so happy you're OK and . . ."

His eyes changed into dark swirls of glacial meltwater.

"I've imprisoned the Mother of All Nightmares back in the dream world," I blurted out.

Mr Curley nodded.

The knight nudged me and I stopped talking. I fished around inside my rucksack for my bottle of DreamDrops and gave it to Mr Curley.

"You can count them, but there's only one missing," I said. I led Bert across the floor, fought my way through the curtains and descended the stairs.

The basement had been put back to the way it was. It was hard to imagine Myrdina had ever been here.

Bert laid his shield and swords on the table and threw himself on the sofa. I took off my rucksack and sat by him.

"Bert, I'm sorry for everything I've put you through. Can you forgive me?"

The knight sighed, the freckle between his Slush Puppie-blue eyes popping up as he scowled. "Not really. I can quite honestly say that coming here has been the worst experience of my life and the only good thing about it is that I get to go home."

"Oh," I said, knotting my hands together on my lap. "I'm going to miss you and Lantern – and Firepuffles a bit. The place isn't going to be the same without you." I wiped my nose.

Bert propped himself up with a cushion that had a tiger on it. "Don't take this the wrong way, but I hope I never see you again, because if I do it means you've been at the DreamDrops and my life will probably be in mortal danger again."

I got to my feet and slung my rucksack on.

I could hear footsteps on the stairs. "Still here, Ollo?" said Mr Curley.

I closed my coat and pulled my hood up. "Give Lantern a goodbye pat from me," I said to Bert. "And Firepuffles too."

"Will do," said the knight.

"Safe home. And you really are brave, Bert," I said. "That wasn't just acting."

"Ollo?" The knight groaned as he got to his feet. "I've got something for you. They must have fallen out of your pocket at Camp de Leon." He handed over the three gold coins that Myrdina had given me.

Grinning at Bert, I squeezed him as hard as I could, which must have hurt because it brought tears to his eyes.

I took one last look at the knight and the basement of the Dream Store before I stole out into the unforgiving night, knowing I could never return.

CHAPTER 17

When I'd made it home after leaving Bert, Lantern and Firepuffles at the Dream Store, I couldn't have been more thankful to discover my parents had been changed back to normal. Dad was asleep in front of the TV and Mum was snoring her head off in bed. From the light that flickered under his door, I could tell Kyle was playing computer games.

It had taken me a while to pluck up the courage to enter my room. I'd never been so happy to find the bed unmade, school books scattered everywhere and clothes all over the floor. I'd closed the wardrobe and climbed into bed, grateful there was a ceiling to shelter me from the pouring rain. I was so tired, I couldn't sleep and lay listening to the wind as it rattled the window. Every now and again the black shape of the curtains would ripple and lift in the draft and I'd sit bolt upright, the nape of my neck damp with sweat, convinced Myrdina had come for me.

The next morning it was obvious that neither Mum nor Dad had any memory of the Mother of All Nightmares, nor of being a spider or a fly. Kyle got up early as usual, so he could finish off the last of the Frosties, and then returned to bed.

When I'd shown Mum and Dad the gold coins, the first thing they'd asked me was where I'd stolen them from. I looked them straight in the eye and said I'd found them in the woods.

Mum had come with me to Cash Converters, where they'd fetched such a good price, we were able to pay off most of our bills.

Dad got himself a new job in a warehouse that preferred humans over machinery. Mum was so happy, the pair of them smooched around the house at every given opportunity, which made me wish on several occasions that they were a spider and a fly again.

I'd passed Roxy Patterson in the corridor on the first morning back at school. She pretended not to notice me, but I saw her fearful glances. It took Bert being scared of everything in Parradicehill to make me realize you have to be your own knight in shining armour. It's better to rescue yourself than wait around for someone else to do it for you because it might never happen.

I stopped trying to be invisible at school and, slowly but surely, people began to notice me for the right reasons. I became friends again with Aiva, Fadumo, Effi, Liam and Brooklyn, who were just as pleased as I was that Roxy Patterson left us alone. I still heard the odd insult echoing around the playing fields and the canteen, but it was less often now there was a story going around that I wasn't to be messed with because I was the one who knocked Roxy Patterson's front tooth out.

I'd smile when I thought about Bert telling me I could give Firepuffles a run for her money. I missed the knight and Lantern, and wondered what adventures they were having in Eldermere Forest without me. I'd become used to the clanking of his armour and the horse snorting; it was deafeningly quiet without them.

I'd visit Seraphina every week. As soon as I'd walk into Little Whispers Café she would check to see if I'd brought a dragon or some other dangerous creature with me. Seraphina had been right about a lot of things, including the deliciousness of the red velvet cake which, once tasted, I couldn't get enough of.

Jeannie had decided she wanted us to go back to being best friends. She'd sidled up to me during art class, wearing the red shoes that matched mine. She'd torn a strawberry lace in half and given me a piece.

"I was only pals with Roxy Patterson so I wouldn't get picked on," she had said. "I never liked her as much as you. You're my best friend." Then she'd chatted away as if nothing had happened. There was a moment where I had longed for us to go back to the way we were, so that my life could feel normal again.

"Hey," Jeannie had said. "We could go to the park and hang out on our bench. Just the two of us."

"No thanks," I had replied. "I'm meeting Ava and Liam at the cinema."

Her face had fallen and she'd spent the rest of the class in a sulk. I wanted to be friends with someone who'd stick by me when the going got tough, not turn against me. I was pleased she was no longer fossilized in stone, but I'd get along just fine without a best friend like her.

Every night, when the moon crept into the window, glowing a million times brighter than the Paulo's Chunky Chicken shop sign, and the stars littered the night sky, I'd think about all the children filling the Book of Dreams with magic and wonder, and pine to be back at the Dream Store with Mr Curley and Sausage. The ache would hurt the soft parts inside me so much, I'd cry myself to sleep.

And then one day, a pineapple-scented letter dropped through the letterbox from Mr Curley, inviting me to the Dream Store for tea and cake.

After a sleepless night, I raced past the wonky

fruit and veg stall, brushed my arm against the red stone wall as I'd turned the corner into Hidden Lane, and skimmed over the cobbles, arriving outside the Dream Store out of breath.

I pressed my nose against the window, marvelling at the display for Deep Sea Adventure DreamDrops. Thousands of rainbow-coloured tropical fish flashed past the bottles, which were hidden in giant clamshells that opened and closed. Every now and again, a shark would cut past in the flick of a tail, its eyes full of menace and its jaws slightly open, showing its raggedy teeth.

There was a part of me that was scared to go back inside because I was ashamed. Ashamed of the awful things that had happened because I'd had a dream.

The bell to the shop tinkled and Mr Curley popped his head out. "Are you intending on joining us today, Ollo?" he asked.

I smiled, then frowned, then bit my lip and finally nodded.

The Dream Store was busy. I lingered for a second, soaking up the excitement and joy. I gazed at the bottles, each one filled to the brim with new friends and adventure.

"Follow me!" roared Mr Curley over the din as he strode across the floor and vanished through the emerald curtains.

I hesitated, a pulse fluttering in my throat.

He held the curtains open.

I'd faced Myrdina and stood up to Roxy Patterson; I could do this.

I meandered my way through the crowd, walked through the curtains and nipped down the wrought-iron steps, breathing in the smell of warm chocolate fudge. As I approached the sofas, I spied a cake on the table so glossy, I could see my reflection in it.

I was about to sit when the room filled with a chorus of cheers. A bird skimmed low over my head, making me duck. Sausage turned gracefully to land on my shoulder, where she purred like a cat as she nipped my earlobe. Being with her again made me realize just how much I'd missed her. After making a huge fuss of her, I sat down and straightened my skirt, fighting the urge to pick at the hem.

"Did Bert, Lantern and Firepuffles make it back to Eldermere Forest OK?" I asked.

"They were returned safely and by all accounts are thriving in A Knight's Adventure."

I smiled, happy Bert was back home being gallant. "I didn't think you'd ever want to see me again, Mr Curley."

He moved a couple of cushions and sat opposite me, crossing his legs. "I should have realized that day when Sausage was making the noise of an alarm, you'd been up to no good."

"*Naughty, naughty. Very naughty,*" cackled Sausage.

"Why did you take the drops, Ollo? Was it because I asked you not to?" Mr Curley sounded more weary than angry.

Sausage stopped purring and tilted her head.

I shifted on the sofa. "I thought if I had a dream the knight could teach me how to defend myself against the school bully."

"The marauding girls in the lane?" he asked.

I nodded and Mr Curley's face relaxed as if something finally made sense to him.

"I've asked you here so I can apologize. I was very angry when I last saw you and not thinking straight."

I stared at Mr Curley, not quite believing my ears.

"You must have been terrified if you felt your only option was to have a dream, which would put you in great danger and risk you losing everything you cared about here," he said.

I puffed a whole winter's worth of wind out my mouth. "I thought the bully was going to kill me."

"Oh, Ollo. I had no idea the situation had become so grave. Please believe me when I say I'm sorry I didn't do more to help you. A Guardian of Dreamers should be able to protect children regardless of whether they are awake or asleep." Mr Curley paused for a moment. "There's something else, Ollo. In my fear of Myrdina becoming real I became a little overzealous in trying to stamp out nightmares. Now that she's safely back in her world, she has just as much right to create her nightmares as I do dreams. To eradicate them completely would be a mistake. They're needed so children can confront their fears and work their way through stressful situations. So, for the moment, while Myrdina is being monitored closely by the Guild of Dreams and Nightmares, I'm going to hold back on the Nightmare Repellent. But it's always there should Myrdina ever try to tip the balance again."

"Mr Curley, I'm sorry for stealing the drops and releasing Myrdina into Parradicehill." I gripped the edges of the seat. "Is something bad going to happen because of what I did?"

He pulled on his earlobe. "I had underestimated her, Ollo. The magic I used to bind her to the cottage was weak and made it easy for her to break free. I suspected it was only a matter of time before Myrdina attempted to escape the dream world again. Few would have shown the courage and determination you did in trying to stop her. If you had failed, all those who had been petrified into stone would have perished. The dream essence you made was inspired, and imprisoning her in a storm cloud a stroke of genius. Children don't like thunder and lightning, so they'll always scarper if they hear her approaching. And with Myrdina being held captive high in the sky, no one will be able to reach her, and the teeth are an extra insurance policy. With very little experience, you created a dream essence that was extremely powerful and effective. I doubt we'll have any more trouble from her, Ollo, and we'll just have to hope when it's time for the next Mother of All Nightmares to be chosen, that she's not as wicked as Myrdina."

"You had every right to be furious with me and have been nothing but understanding," I said. "I am very sorry about what happened."

Mr Curley said nothing.

I was glad we were talking again, but something was playing on my mind. He'd never want me in the shop again because of all the trouble I caused.

I decided it would be better if I left now, before he mentioned this.

I got to my feet.

Mr Curley's white eyebrows lowered. "Do you have somewhere you need to be?"

"No. But you can't possibly give me my job back."

"Why not?"

"Because you'll never be able to trust me around the drops again."

"The shrewdest judges of character I know has forgiven you – and if Sausage can, it would be wise for me to follow suit."

"You're welcome!" Sausage shook her tail feathers.

Mr Curley went over to the window and gazed out into the courtyard. "I simply cannot ignore the aptitude you have for making dreams." He turned to face me. "There's no need for an answer just yet – but Sausage and I would like you to consider coming back to work with us. I'd teach you the basics of weaving dreams, so you'd have a solid understanding of the alchemy required. Sausage will no longer accept Brazil nuts as bribes and would watch you like a hawk. You would be forbidden from entering the Dream Factory and prohibited from practising magic in Dream HQ until such time as I believed it was safe for you to do so."

My mouth opened and shut more than the fish in the Deep Sea Adventure window display.

"I have something to show you, Ollo." Mr Curley opened a cupboard and brought out an object that had been wrapped in tartan tissue paper and tied with string.

He gave it to me. Sausage perched on my shoulder for a closer look.

I undid the string and tore off the paper to find the most beautiful DreamDrops bottle I'd ever seen. The red glass was covered in the characters from all my favourite stories. Its stopper was shaped like an open book and when I pressed it you could hear children laughing. Handwritten on the label was: *A Novel Adventure.*

I gasped. *"You made it into a dream?"*

Mr Curley smiled. "Your ideas are the most extraordinary I've come across. With your help we can think of enthralling ways to keep children entertained." He cast his gaze down to the floor and then back up to me. "The Dream Store isn't the same without you."

My insides felt as though they would burst.

I couldn't keep the answer to myself another second longer.

"Sausage? Mr Curley? I'd love to come back and work at the Dream Store!"

"Knickers!" Sausage took off, zooming around the room exploding like Chinese firecrackers and

scattering her black feathers everywhere.

"Language, Sausage!" Mr Curley's eyes lit up and a pattern of old smile lines appeared on his face. He clasped his hands together, delighted. "This is wonderful news, Ollo."

"Mr Curley?"

"Yes, Ollo?"

"Could I have a slice of the chocolate fudge cake now? I'm starving."

The whoops, shrieks and stamping feet of children drifted through the curtains and floated down the stairs. The bottle of A Novel Adventure caught my eye and a feeling of exhilaration stirred deep inside me. I never wanted to take the DreamDrops again, but if I could create the most fantastical dreams ever seen in the store, I'd be the happiest girl alive.

Mr Curley cut me a huge slice of chocolate fudge cake, placed it on a plate and passed it over to me. As I took a bite, the icing squidged out the sides of the sponge on to my fingers.

The sun appeared in all its glory, shining a spotlight on Mr Curley's possessions as if they were priceless artefacts in a grand museum. I grinned at Mr Curley and Sausage, who sat on the sofa with golden halos of sunshine around their heads. For a moment, in that light, everything took my breath away. It was as if I was having a dream at last – the dream I'd always longed for.

ACKNOWLEDGEMENTS

Edgar Allan Poe said: "Those who dream by day are cognizant of many things which escape those who dream only by night." This book is the end result of an awful lot of dreaming (and writing) by day – and a few sleepless nights. Thanks, Polly, for all your wisdom. You possess an unrivalled imagination, which I've noted is far darker than mine. And thanks, Lauren, for weaving more magic than Mr Curley to make this happen. You are a Guardian of Writers. I'm most grateful to Gen Herr for whipping the entire manuscript into shape and to Pete Matthews for correcting my errors. I salute everyone at Scholastic for working so hard to make *The Night My Dream Came Alive* what it is. I'm such a fan of Beatriz Castro; it really is a dream come true to have her illustrate the cover.

Thank you to Lara, Rodney, Cat, Lisa, Ann Pann, Julie Rea, Catherine Hokin, Pauline Smith, Claire Wadham and the Front Page crew, Helle Norup, Julie Sykes, Fiona Sharp, Scott Evans, Kevin Cobane, Golden Hare Books and Moniack Mhor for your support along the way. Special thanks to George Giles, William Probert and Gail Thomas for your monumental kindness and works of art.

Writing was a dream only made possible by the backing of Scottish Book Trust, who bring the magic of reading and writing to people of all ages. Thank you to Caitrin Armstrong, Lynsey Rogers, Kay Bohan, Will Mackie, Lynsey May, Andrew Blair and Alan Lynch to name but a few. Go on! Help keep this vital work going by donating at scottishbooktrust.com

Finally, hurrah to books for bringing us adventure, laughter, hope, love, friendship and escapism when we need it the most.

Also available from Juliette Forrest:

A brave, bright girl embarks on a heart-racing adventure to find her missing father – with magic and danger quite literally in the air.

"If you only read one book this summer … make it this one." *Guardian*

A thrilling story about a girl who can see the world through a rainbow of colours not visible to others – and the spooky adventure she must go on full of witches, ghosts and other things lurking around the corners of her not-so-ordinary-after-all town...

ABOUT THE AUTHOR

After backpacking around the world, Juliette Forrest worked as both an art director and copywriter for some of the UK's best advertising agencies. She became a Scottish Book Trust New Writer awardee in 2014 and is writer-in-residence at St John Paul II Primary. Juliette lives in Glasgow where she is taken for regular walks by her ex-rescue dog.